Concern ro
continued d

"You must have expected after all you've done that you wouldn't be forgotten when it came time for Aunt Leah to give up her property."

"Please, Aaron." Molly stopped in her tracks. "You mustn't think that. I never did. We all know how Leah felt about family."

"You've been as good as family to her. Better," he said.

She was shaking her head. "I didn't expect anything. I still don't. I just want to do my job. You don't owe me anything. Except my salary, that is." Laughing, she turned, cutting through the brush to the farmyard behind the inn.

Aaron watched her, feeling as if she'd won that round. Except that they weren't fighting a battle, were they? Her slender figure moved through the grass, and she bent gracefully to pat the brown-and-white beagle that rose, tail wagging, from its nap on the porch of the inn.

She baffled him, and he didn't know why. And he had a feeling that he wasn't going to figure it out very easily.

A lifetime spent in rural Pennsylvania and her Pennsylvania Dutch heritage led **Marta Perry** to write about the Plain People who add so much richness to her home state. Marta has seen over seventy of her books published, with over seven million books in print. She and her husband live in a beautiful central Pennsylvania valley noted for its farms and orchards. When she's not writing, she's reading, traveling, baking or enjoying her six beautiful grandchildren.

Books by Marta Perry

Love Inspired

Brides of Lost Creek

Second Chance Amish Bride
The Wedding Quilt Bride
The Promised Amish Bride
The Amish Widow's Heart
A Secret Amish Crush
Nursing Her Amish Neighbor
The Widow's Bachelor Bargain
Match Made at the Amish Inn

An Amish Family Christmas
"Heart of Christmas"
Amish Christmas Blessings
"The Midwife's Christmas Surprise"

Visit the Author Profile page at LoveInspired.com for more titles.

MATCH MADE AT THE AMISH INN

MARTA PERRY

LOVE INSPIRED
INSPIRATIONAL ROMANCE

LOVE INSPIRED®
INSPIRATIONAL ROMANCE

ISBN-13: 978-1-335-93707-0

Match Made at the Amish Inn

Copyright © 2025 by Martha P. Johnson

Recycling programs for this product may not exist in your area.

Love Inspired
22 Adelaide St. West, 41st Floor
Toronto, Ontario M5H 4E3, Canada
www.LoveInspired.com

Printed in Lithuania

MIX
Paper | Supporting
responsible forestry
FSC® C021394

Charity suffereth long, and is kind;
charity envieth not; charity vaunteth not itself,
is not puffed up, Doth not behave itself unseemly,
seeketh not her own, is not easily provoked,
thinketh no evil; Rejoiceth not in iniquity, but
rejoiceth in the truth; Beareth all things, believeth
all things, hopeth all things, endureth all things.
—*1 Corinthians* 13:4–7

To my dear husband, who always supports me,
and to our precious family, who brighten our lives.

Chapter One

"Molly Esch, if you don't stop fussing over this room for a child you don't even know, I'm going to scream."

Having known Hilda since they were in first grade together at the Amish school, Molly felt sure that Hilda would do no such thing, but now that Hilda was working for her at the Amish Inn, she'd reverted to talking like that sassy six-year-old she'd been. And Hilda wouldn't be content until she had an answer.

"Think of it," Molly said, frowning at the patchwork quilt on the single bed. She'd love to find something more suited to a little girl. "Poor little thing is only eight, and she's lost her mother and she and her daadi are moving to a strange place. I want it to be welcoming for her."

"Ach, I understand that." Hilda's face softened with sympathy. "Poor child," she echoed. "But what about the father? You haven't said a thing about why Leah Fisher wants to bring in this stranger to manage the inn when you've been helping her for over two years and could do it perfectly fine all by yourself. So tell me!"

Hilda's eyes sparkled with curiosity and her normally sharp voice demanded answers. Everything about Hilda had always been sharp, from her pointed nose to her high voice to her curiosity about anyone and everyone in the community of Lost Creek.

No wonder Hilda wanted to know. Leah Fisher *had* been Molly's friend all her life and her mentor during the two years since Molly's life had crumbled around her. Why had Leah decided to bring in this stranger to take charge of the inn while Leah recovered from her accident?

Leah doesn't trust you to do it. That critical voice in the back of her mind had been unusually active since her intended husband had run off the very night before their wedding.

Leah had been a rock at the time. In the midst of all the gossip and sympathy and wondering, Leah, her mother's dearest friend, had appeared with the most helpful suggestion—that Molly should come and work with her in running the Amish Inn.

Molly had to smile at Leah's idea of a cure for a broken heart—work, challenge and more work. But it had turned out just as her mother and Leah had expected. Learning all the ins and outs of running the busy inn and catering to the mostly Englisch visitors had given her a new interest in life. Gradually Leah had put more and more of the actual management into Molly's hands, challenging her, and Molly had been so occupied that she hadn't had time to mourn over William's defection to the outside world.

Molly had thought Leah had confidence in her, and her own self-confidence, battered as it had been, had begun to come back. But now, when Leah had to turn the management over to someone else while her badly broken legs healed, she'd brought in her husband's nephew to do it instead of relying on Molly.

She doesn't trust you. Molly wondered if hitting her

head against the stairwell wall would quiet that voice in her mind. Dismissing the impulse, she and Hilda went down the back stairway of the inn's annex, where the owner lived. Maybe Hilda had given up on her questioning, but she doubted it.

"Well?" Hilda demanded as they emerged into the kitchen from the narrow stairway. "Why is she bringing in this Aaron Fisher?"

Molly shrugged, knowing she had to say something or Hilda would never go home. Aaron Fisher and his little daughter would be here before long, and she needed a few minutes to tidy herself.

But it looked as if she wasn't going to get them. The front doorbell rang, and then Leah called out to her.

"Molly, they're here!" Leah sounded so excited that Molly knew she had to move fast before Leah was trying to get out of bed.

"I'll be right there," Molly called. She shoved Hilda out the back door with questions still on her lips. "I'll tell you when I figure it out," she said. "See you tomorrow."

She closed the door on Hilda's protests, dusted off her apron and tidied her hair as best she could. Then she hurried toward the front door, where the bell was ringing again.

She risked a glance out the front window to see an Englisch driver unloading suitcases and bags from a station wagon, while an Amishman and child stood on the porch. Yah, that would be Aaron Fisher. Now she had to wilkom him and act as if nothing at all was wrong. Taking a deep breath, she arranged a smile on her face and opened the door.

Molly decided she might as well not have bothered about the smile, since the man who must be Aaron Fisher clearly didn't. In fact, his face wore no expression at all. If he was glad to be here, it didn't show.

Still, she recognized him. She'd seen him long ago, when Aaron had visited his aunt and uncle as a teenager, and she'd been a little girl tagging along with her mother. Then he'd looked…superior, she decided. At that point, she hadn't dared to talk to him.

But times had changed. She slid a strand of bronze hair back under her kapp. One thing about having red hair—folks usually remembered you. But it seemed that Aaron didn't.

"Wilkom, Aaron." She infused a little extra pleasure into her voice to make up for the fact that she didn't feel it. He was looking back toward the driver and the luggage and didn't immediately respond. In fact, he almost seemed to look past the driver, toward the place he'd left. She felt a surge of sympathy that surprised her.

"Please, come in," she said, gesturing to the hallway of the annex. "And this must be Rebecca." She bent to bring her face on the level of the eight-year-old, who edged behind her father, holding onto his black coat. "Do you like to be called Becky?"

She didn't get a smile. The child's bright blue eyes just stared at her warily. The freckled little face seemed made for laughter, not for the solemn expression it wore now.

Still, she guessed there was no reason why a motherless eight-year-old should be happy about yet another change in her short life. After a moment, the little girl gave the slightest nod.

Relieved, Molly smiled again as she straightened, but Aaron's expression, or lack of it, hadn't changed. "Is that my aunt?" he asked abruptly.

Yanked back to the here and now, Molly realized she was hearing the tinkling sound of the small bell Leah used to let her know she wanted something.

"Yah, they're here," she called out. "Do you want them to come to you first, before dealing with the luggage?"

Leah's cheerful laugh sounded. "For sure. I need a hug from my kinfolk."

"Right away, then." She pointed to the open door that led to the former dining room, now converted into a room for a recuperating patient.

"Your aunt is just in there. Do you want—"

He didn't let her finish. Holding his child's hand, he took a long step toward the door. "Tell the driver to put things on the porch. I'll be there to help him in a moment."

Not even a please. Somehow, she didn't think Aaron had changed much from that superior teenager who hadn't seemed to see anything he liked in Lost Creek.

She watched as the tall broad-shouldered man and the tiny child walked away from her. At the last second before entering the other room, Becky turned her head and gave Leah a shy, sweet smile.

She was such a pushover for a child, Molly told herself. Not the father—she could do without him. But she promptly lost her heart to the lonely little girl.

Aaron followed his daughter's gaze for a moment, noticing her slight smile. If Becky warmed up to Aunt Leah's helper, that would be more than he'd hoped for. But he didn't have time to think about it now. The woman vanished on her errand, and Aaron turned to find Aunt Leah holding out her arms to him.

He hurried to hug her, but he was shocked. He'd always

seen Aunt Leah as an energetic, positive woman, busy every
minute of the day. To find her leaning back on her pillows,
looking helpless, struck him in the heart. He managed to
smile as he pulled away, and she clung to him as if she
didn't want to let go. Then her hands slipped away, and he
patted her cheek.

"Ach, it's been too long. I've missed you so very much."

"Me, too," he murmured, thinking about the clash between his father and Aunt Leah's husband. How any two
brothers could have been so different, he didn't know, but
it had created a chasm between the two families. Maybe
now that breach could be healed.

"I know." Aunt Leah seemed to understand exactly what
he thought. "They were too different in so many ways, but
they were certain sure alike in their stubborn insistence
that they were right."

"They were, always." He looked back with sorrow at the
split between the families. Everyone had been hurt by it,
but his daad and his onkel never seemed to see it.

"Well, they're both gone now," Aunt Leah said with some
of her usual spirit. "Their quarrel died with them, and they're
at peace. It's time to move on."

"You're right," he said firmly. He wouldn't hold onto a
grudge he'd never understood.

"I wanted to find a way to get you here, but I didn't count
on this." She gestured to the bulky casts on both her legs.

"No, that's certain sure." He sat back in the chair by the
bed, holding Becky in the curve of his arm. "How did it
happen?"

"Ach, I was foolish, that's certain sure. Molly told me not
to venture down the cellar steps, but I didn't listen to her."

She made a face. "It was a long way to that cement floor. If Molly had already left, I'd have been down there all night."

"It sounds as if you should have listened to her advice." Surely, that woman could have prevented Leah's foolishness if she'd tried.

"I was never very good at heeding advice," she said, her soft cheeks crinkling in a smile. "Anyway, I'm wonderful glad you were able to come. I was so afraid you wouldn't be able to."

Her letter had actually been a gift from the Lord to Aaron, though she couldn't know it. It had given him a reason to leave behind the place where his wife had died, the place that reminded him of his loss every second of every day.

"It was the best thing that could have happened for us." He gave Becky a little hug. "We were ready to be somewhere for a fresh start. Right, Becky?"

He looked at her sweet face. It used to be so lively and energetic, filled with happiness and curiosity. Now it seemed he couldn't find the child she'd been. She'd pulled back into a shell, and he hadn't been able to reach her. Maybe now it would be different.

Maybe. Right now it didn't seem likely, but there was time—time to get used to a new place, new people, relatives who would love her.

Aunt Leah gave an understanding smile, as if she understood everything he didn't say.

At that moment, there was a light tap on the door, which stood open. The woman his aunt had called Molly hesitated there, as if wondering if she were welcome.

"I'm sure you have lots to catch up on, but I wondered if Becky would like to see her new bedroom and put some of her things away." Her smile was for Becky.

"I don't think…" he began, sure that Becky wouldn't go anywhere without him. To his astonishment, she pulled away from the circle of his arm, nodding. He touched her shoulder. "Are you sure?"

Becky nodded vigorously.

"Yah, all right, then. You mind what Molly says now."

She nodded and went carefully around the bed to take the hand Molly held out to her. With a quick glance backward, she hurried out of the room. He could hear their steps on the stairs and the light sounds of their voices. He pictured them talking to each other, Molly's green eyes sparkling. That dark red hair like the center of a flame… Where had he seen it before?

Aunt Leah laughed a little. "You're surprised, ain't so?"

"I am surprised," he responded. "Becky never warms up to new people that fast. At least not since her mammi passed."

"Ach, it's a hard thing for a child her age. But you'll see. Molly is good with people, especially kinder. And she knows everything about the inn. Anything you want to know, Molly can tell you." She leaned back on the pillows as if fatigue had swept over her.

"This has been too much for you," he said, clamping down his irritation toward Molly, who knew everything. "Why don't you rest?"

"No, no," Aunt Leah said, though she did look tired. "There's something else I must tell you."

"Maybe later, when you're rested," he suggested.

"No, now." She gripped his hand. "There's something I must say so you'll understand why I wanted you to come now."

He patted her hand. "It's all right. I understand. You wanted some family here to help."

She smiled, her head moving restlessly against the pillow. "Not just that. You have to understand what we planned."

"We?"

"Your Onkel Isaiah," she said firmly. "We talked it over long ago, when we knew we weren't going to have any kinder of our own." Her face seemed drawn for a moment. "It was a grief to us, but there was you. Isaiah's own nephew, and such a fine, loving boy. We decided then that when we were gone, the Amish Inn would belong to you."

It took a few moments for the words to sink in. He'd accepted that she'd needed him during this emergency, but he'd never expected anything like this, especially after the brothers' quarrel.

"You don't mean it," he said. Wondering what exactly he felt about it. If his dear Rachel were still alive…

"Ach, I know exactly what I mean." Her voice was strong. "It was my wish as well as Isaiah's. I just never thought the time would come so soon."

"But you'll get well," he said quickly. "You'll be fine, and you can take charge again. I'll stay as long as you need me, but you can't just give it up. I know how much the inn means to you."

"Yah, it does, but I'm getting tired. I think it's time to ease off a bit. Even if I get back to how I was before the accident, I'd want that. Maybe we'll do it together for a few years. But I'll step back and let you take over."

Aaron still couldn't find the right words. Now that he began to get used to the idea, he found it was increasingly appealing. A thriving business was nothing to turn down.

It would be a challenge, but he could feel himself rising to meet it.

"But what about Molly?" he said suddenly. "Wouldn't she be expecting something after working with you?"

"There will be something for Molly, if everything works out." Aunt Leah's lips quirked in a smile, and she seemed to be looking into the future. "I know it. And what do you say?"

Aaron held his breath for a moment, feeling his head spin. If this was what his aunt wanted, how could he turn away from a secure future for his daughter? He let out a long breath. "Yah, all right. If it's what you really want."

Becky held onto Molly's hand on the way up the stairs to the second floor, and the closer they got to the top, the tighter her grip became. Molly looked down at the top of the child's head, seeing the silky hair parted in the middle and drawn back under a snowy kapp. Even the top of her head seemed to announce her tension.

Deciding she'd better break the silence, Molly gestured toward the space around them, where they could glance down at the hall. "This part of the house is called the annex. It's where your Aunt Leah lives. And you, too, now that you're here. The big part in front is where the visitors stay."

Did the child understand? Most eight-year-olds here in Lost Creek would know what she meant, but it was all strange to Becky.

"A lot of strangers?" she asked, looking up at her, and her eyes were wide. A little afraid, Molly thought, of all those Englischers she was imagining.

She paused, turning to smile down at the child. "You know what your Aunt Leah always says? She says strangers are just friends you haven't met yet. All our visitors turn out to be friends."

Becky seemed to puzzle that over in her mind. "Why do they?"

"Mostly because they like it here. And also because your Aunt Leah is so friendly. When she smiles, no one can help but smile back." It occurred to Molly that Becky had only seen her elderly aunt lying in a bed with lines of strain on her face. That hadn't been a good example, she guessed. She tried to think of something else the child might respond to.

"This is the second floor, where the bedrooms are." Molly couldn't help herself… She was eager to see how Becky reacted to her new bedroom. She and Hilda had done their best to make it welcoming to a child.

"See, this first room is usually Aunt Leah's, but she had to move downstairs when she hurt her legs. The next one is for your daadi." She pushed the door farther open and gestured toward the double bed with the patchwork quilt.

Turning, she led Molly across the hall. "And right across from daadi's room is a bedroom just for you." She flung open the door, hoping the room was as appealing to a child as she'd tried to make it.

But Becky wasn't looking inside. Instead, she gazed at Molly…looking a little lonely, it seemed to her. "But where do you sleep?"

Molly took her hand again, touched by this sign of friendship. "I usually sleep at home, where my mammi and daadi and the rest of the family live. But sometimes I stay here, in case your Aunt Leah needs something in the night."

"Oh." Still a bit of disappointment in her face, and Molly wondered again what was going on in Becky's mind.

Molly led her into the bedroom. "When I was a little

girl, I sometimes would sleep here, in the bed you have. My mammi worked at the inn, and she'd bring me with her. So if it was late, she'd tuck me up in this comfy bed." She pressed down on the mattress, and a moment later Becky did the same, seeming to assess its softness.

"You know the story about the three bears?"

Becky nodded, leaning against the end of the bed. "Mammi used to tell me that story." Her lower lip quivered, but then she firmed it, and Molly pretended not to notice.

"I always thought this bed was like the one belonging to Baby Bear. Just right. Maybe it'll be just right for you."

Becky's lips twitched, and then it happened—she smiled. The smile lit her small face with life and enjoyment, and it warmed Molly's heart. That was exactly what she'd hoped for. She could only pray that nothing would happen to disturb the fragile friendship that had sprung up between them.

Becky patted the bed again, and then looked around. "Where do my dresses go?"

"We should have some hooks up for clothes, ain't so? But we have something else here." She ran her fingers down the chair rail molding on the wall and then put Becky's hand on the latch that was almost invisible against the wood. "Just push down on that and see what you find."

For an instant the child looked wary, as if fearing an unpleasant surprise, but then she seemed to gain encouragement from Molly's smile. She pressed, and the door swung open showing the closet with hooks for clothing. The side wall was lined with shelves, and on them were a few books and toys that Molly had brought from home.

Becky's lips formed a silent, *Oh*, as she looked at the faceless Amish doll who wore a neat kapp that matched her own and a green dress with a white apron. She looked at Molly with a silent question, and Molly nodded.

"She's for you." Molly lifted her down. "I always thought some little girl might stay here who needed a friend. So that's why she's for you." She smiled, first at the doll and then at Becky, who giggled. Her arms closed around the doll, and then she hesitated.

"For sure?" she asked.

Molly laughed. "For sure. I always called her Maggie, but you can give her another name if you want."

"Maggie," Becky said softly, and hugged the doll close to her heart.

It was a perfect moment, Molly thought. Becky felt welcomed, just as she'd hoped. As for Aaron and the inn—

A deep voice spoke from the doorway. "I thought you were up here unpacking."

Molly tried to hang onto her moment of pleasure, but it slipped away in the withering effect of Aaron's frown. She pinned a smile to her face.

"We're in no hurry. I want to show Becky all the special things about this room that I found when I was her age."

Meanwhile, Becky was tugging at her father's coat. "That's my bed. Molly used to sleep in it sometimes, and she said it was like Baby Bear's bed—just right."

Aaron bent over his daughter, and for a moment Molly couldn't guess what he was thinking. But then he straightened, holding her in his arms, and they smiled at each other, bringing to life a surprising likeness that she hadn't seen before. Her heart seemed to swell in her chest, and for an instant she couldn't breathe.

Then Aaron turned to her, his frown returning. "I'm sure you have other work to do."

They stood there staring at each other. Did he realize how rude that sounded? She couldn't tell. His expression didn't give away his feelings, assuming he had any.

She would do what Leah had asked her to do. But she really couldn't believe that this situation was going to turn out well for her, not when she had to work with...no, work for...a man like this.

Chapter Two

Why did Leah bring in Aaron Fisher? Molly found that Hilda's question kept repeating in her thoughts as she went back downstairs and through the hallway to the inn. She had several guest rooms to freshen up in preparation for visitors in a couple of days. That should give her a little thinking time. Once the tourists started coming for the autumn color, there'd be no time for anything but to keep up.

Hardly noticing what she was doing, she went up the gracious staircase that served the inn itself, running her hand along the highly polished railing. The afternoon sun sent colors through the stained-glass window at the top, and she lingered to admire it. And then she found that her mind had tumbled back to the same place. Aaron was Leah's late husband's kin. Despite the fact that Leah hadn't seen him for years, she'd sent for him to take over management of the inn instead of trusting Molly. No matter how she added it up, Molly still came up with the same answer. Leah didn't trust her to handle it.

Molly realized she'd been standing in the same spot, staring at colors reflecting on the carpet as if she wanted to change the pattern for at least ten minutes. *Not helping,* she scolded herself. She ought to tackle the problem logically. What did she actually know about Aaron Fisher?

Not much. Leah had been secretive about her thoughts and her plans since the accident. Molly's mother might know more—she and Leah had always been close, but if so, she hadn't shared with Molly.

Molly had that vague memory of a superior-looking teenager, coupled with the fact that he was now a widower with a small child. Before she could figure out how to work with him, she'd have to know more. Otherwise, she risked stepping into one pothole after another, saying all the wrong things. Leah would have to talk.

Another fifteen minutes and she was ready to go with the rooms clean and ready except for tomorrow's flowers. She'd best check in on Leah. Molly stiffened her backbone, but her determination turned out not to be needed. As soon as she entered Leah's room, Leah reached out a hand to her.

"Ach, Molly, just the person I wanted to see. We need to talk." Propped up against her stacked pillows, her gray hair still neatly tucked under her kapp the way Molly had fixed it this morning, Leah seemed to have regained a little of her normal color. Perhaps she had taken a short nap after talking with her nephew. She seemed to need more catnaps these days.

"Just what I was thinking." Molly scooted a chair closer to the bed. "I need to know a little more about—"

"About Aaron," Leah finished for her. "Yah, for sure you do. And I need to tell you." She paused, as if thinking her way back through the years, choosing what to share. "First off, Aaron's father was my Isaiah's younger brother. You maybe knew that, but you probably didn't know that the two brothers always seemed to be at odds." She shrugged.

"Maybe they were just too much alike—both as stubborn as the day is long."

Molly nodded to show she understood, but she was wondering what this ancient history had to do with today's problems.

"Aaron was the first of his generation in the family, and as it turned out, the only one." Sorrow creased her face for a moment, and Molly knew why. The grief of Leah's life had been the fact that she had no child of her own.

Leah shook her head, as if shaking off those painful memories. "So Isaiah always said that if the inn was a success, we would leave it to Aaron." She hesitated, and then went on, studying Molly's face. "I'm bound by that promise, and it's always been my wish, as well, for the inn to stay in the family. But I'll need your help to make it happen."

"For sure," Molly said quickly. "I understand. And I'll help all I can. I promise." At least it wasn't a question of her competence or of Leah's trust in her. Leah was counting on her to prepare Aaron for his inheritance.

Relief swept through her, but it was tinged with a fear of inadequacy. It wasn't that she doubted her knowledge where running the inn was concerned. But how could she help Aaron if he didn't listen to a word she said?

Leah was already sweeping on. "Isaiah and I thought that as Aaron grew, we'd teach him gradually how to run things, but we didn't count on Isaiah's quarrel with his brother taking off the way it did." She shook her head gravely. "Mind, it was Isaiah's fault, too, but neither of them would give an inch. If only…"

She let that trail off, seeming to drift into thoughts of the past. At last, she sucked in a deep breath and gave Molly a determined look. "Ach, it's no use dwelling on what we ought to have done. We just must pick up and move on. That's what I must do, with your help, ain't so?"

"I'll do my best." She'd best air her concerns now. "You'll have to help me because I don't know Aaron very well. He probably doesn't see any good reason why he should listen to me."

Leah nodded. "Poor boy," she murmured. "Ach, I wish I'd seen him more often. He's changed so much since his wife died, and I've missed it all."

"It's been what? A year or two?" Molly remembered hearing Leah talk about it, but since she hadn't known them, it hadn't made much impression on her.

"Just about a year and a half, I think." Leah's forehead wrinkled in an effort to clear her thoughts, something that seemed more difficult since her accident. "Yah, it was in the early spring last year. It's hard, not having more family. His father had passed, and his mother moved to Ohio to live with her sister."

"That's unusual...for an Amish person not to have family around to help them, I mean," Molly said. "Especially hard for a father left alone with a child." She found herself picturing Becky's sad little face and how it lit up at the sight of her daadi.

They must have a good relationship together, didn't they? Perhaps Aaron just didn't know how to help Becky with her grief. That happened, sometimes.

"I blame myself," Leah said. "I should have invited them to come here right after it happened. I could have helped. Even if Aaron held on to his father's grudge against us, I should..."

"Aren't you the person who just told me not to look at

the past?" Molly patted her hand. "Just pick up the day's burden and move ahead, yah?"

For a moment, Molly feared she'd offended her, but then Leah chuckled softly. "That's right, Molly. You just quote my own words back to me whenever I need to hear them." She squeezed Molly's hand. "You're just like your mammi, with a heart full of love."

A heart full of love that Will hadn't wanted, Molly found herself thinking. She wasn't a good person to help someone else grieving a lost love, but she seemed to be the only one handy. It was certain sure Leah thought she could do it.

Her thoughts slid off in another direction. "After a year and a half, well... I'd think there might be someone else in Aaron's community looking to step into his wife's place."

"For sure, there must be," Leah said. "But Aaron seems to have closed himself off from anyone who might care for him and Becky." She shook her head, staring absently at their linked hands. "Just remember that I'm relying on you."

A sound from behind her made Molly take a glance in that direction. Aaron stood in the doorway. He stared at her with a look as cold as an icicle.

Aaron froze where he stood. How could he freeze, when inside a fire was raging? They'd been talking about him, that was obvious. About his Rachel. He wouldn't have believed it of Aunt Leah. As for Molly, he didn't know enough to say, but not his aunt.

"Komm." Aunt Leah gestured to him, urging him inside. "We were just talking about how we can make Becky feel at home. Molly knows more about eight-year-olds than I do, so she'll be a big help."

He stepped forward, but it wasn't so easy to thaw. "I'm

not looking for help." He cut off the words, hoping his tone would discourage both of them from meddling.

"Ach, Aaron, you never know what you might come to need," Aunt Leah seemed unembarrassed at being caught talking about him, and he suspected she wouldn't be easy to discourage.

She was his kin. Did he really want to discourage her? The answer was obviously no. He'd longed to have family around since Rachel died. Well, now he did, and he was reminded that it had its drawbacks.

He forced himself to smile and steered the talk firmly in a different direction. "I came in to talk to my aunt about school for my daughter," he said. "If you'll excuse us…"

Maybe Aunt Leah wasn't embarrassed, but Molly's cheeks were flushed. "Yah, I have things to do."

She looked glad to escape, but his aunt's voice stopped her.

"No, stay here, Molly."

Molly sent him an apologetic look and came back.

"As I said, Molly knows what's what where eight-year-olds are concerned. And she certain sure knows more about the Amish school. Don't you, Molly?"

"I don't know about that, but I do have four younger brothers and sisters, including eight-year-old twins. I guess I can answer any questions you have. With all the talking our Dora does, I should know a lot."

"Dora is the girl twin," Aunt Leah explained, her lips twitching. "She's a real chatterbox."

His face twisted as he tried to smile. Becky had been a chatterbox, too, but not now. Not since she lost her mammi.

Aaron realized suddenly that Molly's eyes were focused on his face, and they were filled with understanding and caring. For a moment, he was disoriented. She couldn't know what he was thinking, could she?

"I'm sure Dora would like to be Becky's friend and show her the school," Molly said. "Maybe we could get them together over the weekend."

"Maybe," he said slowly, reluctant to commit himself. "But first I want to visit the school and talk to the teacher about my daughter." He didn't mean to sound ungrateful, did he? It seemed to come out that way.

Once again, his aunt rushed in with the answers. He didn't remember her being quite so bossy when Onkel Isaiah was alive.

"That will work out fine," she said. "Tomorrow morning, Hilda will be here helping, so Molly can show you the way to school and introduce you to the teacher." She grimaced. "No one will let me be alone anymore. Makes me feel like a baby."

He was about to say something sympathetic, but Molly just smiled. "If you insist on trying to go down the cellar steps—"

"Ach, I know, I know." Aunt Leah chuckled. "Molly won't let me feel sorry for myself, either."

"Doctor's orders," Molly said brightly. "No moping allowed, according to Dr. Wainwright."

"He sounds like he understands my aunt." Aaron tried to share their gentle teasing, and it wiped out some of the discomfort that had been in the air. "If Molly says it's okay with her, then we'll go chat with the teacher tomorrow."

He certain sure didn't need Molly's help to talk to the Amish school teacher, but it was simpler to agree than to dispute it. Aunt Leah was probably fretting about all the things she couldn't do, like going to the schoolhouse with him tomorrow.

He hesitated, but there was something else on his mind that he ought to work on. "Now that we have that settled, how about letting me pitch in with what needs to be done here? That's why I came, ain't so?"

"We don't have any visitors coming until Saturday." Aunt Leah looked perplexed. "What else would you do?"

"Anything." He waved his hand. "I've learned how to cook a little, and I can clean." He picked up the calendar that was propped on the bedside table. "I see Molly is written in for tonight, but there's no need for her to stay. I'll do whatever needs doing."

He wasn't sure what he'd said, but his aunt and Molly both stared at him for a moment. Then Aunt Leah's lips twitched. "Molly, take him away and explain. I'm ready to have a little nap."

He opened his mouth to argue, but Molly took his arm firmly and led him out of the room, saying, "Have a good rest."

Just before the door closed completely, he distinctly heard a giggle from the direction of the bed. He swung toward Molly, to find her laughing, too.

"What is so funny?" He was on the edge of being offended. They were laughing at him, ain't so?

"Ach, Aaron, don't look so solemn." Molly managed to control her laughter, but her eyes still twinkled. "It's just that the person who stays for the night has to help Leah bathe and get ready for bed and so on. It doesn't matter how much she loves you, but she doesn't want you doing that."

"Oh, right." A flow of red washed up to her cheeks, and suddenly he was smiling, too. They stood there for a moment, laughing together, and he felt the barrier between them had crumbled to dust.

* * *

The next morning, Aaron seemed filled with energy and eager to get off to the schoolhouse. Molly tried to look equally enthusiastic, but she suspected her tiredness showed through. She'd slept on the camp bed set up in the corner of Leah's room, but *slept* hadn't exactly been the right word for it. What with listening for Leah, ready to jump up at her call and thinking about how she would deal with Aaron over the coming weeks, she hadn't actually spent much of the night sleeping.

She finished washing the breakfast dishes and hung the damp towel over the rack. The inn would go to Aaron when Leah was ready to let it go—that was plain. Well, that was what anyone would expect. He was her husband's only relative.

That was as it should be. The little Leah had told her about Aaron's marriage had increased her sympathy for both Aaron and his daughter. Theirs had been a true love match—what she had thought she had with William. It hurt her heart just to think about Aaron's loss, but it was pointless to say that she knew how he felt. She didn't, and if Leah thought she knew what to say in comfort, she was on the wrong track. Leah herself would be far better at that.

Molly leaned against the windowsill and spotted Aaron coming from the barn to the house. She realized, watching him from a distance, that he was huskier than either her closest brother or her daad. A bit taller, too, she'd guess, with a sturdy frame that looked strong enough for anything. She remembered hearing Leah say that he'd worked construction before his wife died. He looked more suited to that than to managing the inn.

He'd obviously finished the chores, and he'd be eager

to get off to the school. But not until Hilda arrived, she reminded herself. They couldn't go off and leave Becky alone with Leah.

Her thoughts were interrupted by Becky coming in from her great-aunt's room. She was carrying a child's teapot, and she held it up to Molly.

"Aunt Leah says can you put some tea in my teapot?" Becky asked. "We're going to have a tea party when you and Daadi go to school."

She looked a little doubtful about the whole thing, making Molly wonder if they were in for tears when Daadi tried to leave without her.

"Yah, of course. I'll fix it for you." This was probably Leah's idea of distracting the child, and she smiled down at the little girl. "Would you like to have some snicker-doodles, too?"

Becky's eyes lit up. "If that's okay. Do you think Aunt Leah would like them?"

"I'll tell you a secret," she said, taking the lid off the cookie jar. "Snickerdoodles are your Aunt Leah's favorite cookies. My mamm made these for her."

"They're my favorite, too," Becky whispered. "I'm good at keeping secrets."

Denke, Lord, Molly murmured in her heart, glad that even something as simple as a favorite cookie brought a smile to that solemn little face.

Aaron came in just then, holding the door for Hilda, who was chattering away a mile a minute. For an instant, Molly regretted not having Hilda's gift of gab, but seeing the slightly dazed expression on Aaron's face, she thought the better of it. She'd rather be herself, she decided.

Hilda jumped right into the tea-party plan. She enlisted

Aaron's help to move a small table next to Leah's bed, and she and Becky drew up the chairs. Molly brought the teapot and plate of cookies, eyeing Becky to be sure she wasn't getting upset, but she seemed completely engrossed in the tea party. Such a good idea of Leah's, as if she knew instinctively that this was the right thing to do. Perhaps it had been something Becky's mother did with her.

But Leah had always been like that, seeming to know what a child needed. It was so sad that God had not blessed her with a houseful of her own.

She lingered, but Aaron gestured to her impatiently. As soon as they were out of the room, he grasped her arm and hustled her out the back door. His long strides ate up the ground, and Molly had to hurry to keep up with him. Finally, she just stopped. He turned to look at her in annoyance, but then his expression faded into a smile.

"Was I rushing you?" he asked, not looking in the least sorry.

"Just a bit," she said, setting a more moderate pace. "Besides, you were about to go the wrong way."

Aaron flushed a bit, looking annoyed again. He didn't like to be caught in a mistake, she guessed.

Ignoring it, she pointed to the path beyond the barn that led down to a farm lane. "The children aren't allowed to go along the road. This path leads into the lane. It winds along parallel to the road and ends up at the school."

· "Without crossing the road?" He gave a short nod. "Good idea." After a few minutes of walking, he spoke again, sounding more normal now. "Tell me about the school. And the teacher. You went there, ain't so?"

"Well, I went there, so I think it's great, of course. But I would, wouldn't I?" She smiled, inviting him with a look to respond with something about his school, but he didn't respond, so she went on.

Matching her steps to his, Molly told him about the school-house. She knew it so well after her years there, but it was surprisingly hard to describe it to someone else. Maybe she still saw it with a child's eyes.

"The teacher has changed now, of course. It's Teacher Grace, one of the Miller family. She finished school just a year before I did, and she's been teaching for several years." Molly hesitated. "She's good, you know. Kind and gentle in spirit, but able to control the most obstreperous boys with a look and a word."

"Even all the red-headed Esch children?" he asked, teasing a little and making her lips quirk.

"Yah, even them. Matthew, he's the next brother after me—he could usually talk his way out of anything, but not with Teacher Grace. She saw right through him." She chuckled. "We enjoyed that."

It wasn't a long walk to the schoolhouse, but it was a pleasant one with willow trees and river birch shading the path. On a warm day like this one, with Aaron trying to be nice, Molly actually enjoyed it despite her initial reluctance.

Just now he was looking between the trees to the right, where a few scattered houses gave way to pastureland. A few placid looking Herefords raised their heads to look at them before going back to munching.

Molly pointed. "Our farm is the next place off to the left."

He didn't seem interested, so she went on. "There's the school, on the right." Molly turned onto the well-worn path, very conscious of Aaron right behind her. "Teacher Grace will be delighted to have a new scholar, especially one starting so early in the school year."

"I'm more worried about how Becky will take it. She's always liked school, but going to a new place might be different." His voice seemed lower, and she glanced back at him as the path came out on the lawn around the schoolhouse. She saw worry tightening the lines around his eyes and tried to sound optimistic.

"Don't borrow trouble. My daad always says that when my mamm gets het up about something. I didn't understand when I was younger, but I grew to think it's good advice."

His face was still set. "Yah, but it's easier said than done."

"I know," Molly said gently, wishing she saw some softening in his expression. "But if she liked school before, surely she will still like it now. And my little sister Dorie is determined to be her very best friend."

Aaron managed a smile. "Denke, Molly."

Maybe she should warn him about Dorie, who talked even faster than Hilda, if that was possible. But he'd soon see. They reached the steps to the white frame schoolhouse, and Molly paused and turned to him. "They'll be having morning recess in a few minutes, so that will be a good time to talk to Teacher Grace. We'll just wait in the back until then." Since he seemed to accept that, she opened the door and they slipped inside.

Teacher Grace glanced up with a quick smile and continued pointing out something on a map to the older scholars while the younger ones practiced printing their letters. A wave of remembering swept over Molly as they stood waiting at the back. Nothing much had changed over the years, with the same maps pinned up on the board, the same rows of wooden desks and even what looked like the same yellow and orange paper leaves pinned around the calendar on the bulletin board.

Molly glanced at Aaron and saw him picking out the three redheads in the classroom—Dorie and David, the eight-year-old twins, and Lida, the eleven-year-old. Lida kept her eyes on the teacher, but Dorie and David stole a quick glance at Molly, and Dorie wiggled, as if finding it hard to sit still. Molly gave a tiny shake of the head to her little sister, not wanting to be embarrassed.

Fortunately, the lesson soon came to an end. Teacher Grace put her pointer down unhurriedly, smiling at her pupils. "I'm going to dismiss you for recess in just a moment, but first I want to remind you to be on your best behavior. We have guests today. No, don't stare at them," she ordered as heads swiveled. "Just put your things away and then file out, youngest grades first."

A soft buzz of conversation rose, and Aaron stepped back as the first and second graders came down the center aisle, the boys jostling each other and the girls chattering. Molly moved to the side, hoping Aaron wouldn't get trampled.

Dorie burst out of the crowd, headed for her, stepping on other scholars' feet as she came. As soon as she was close enough, she grabbed Molly's hand and clung tight. Words burst out of her.

"Molly, do you know what Sally Byler said? She said that her brother William was coming back! I told her he couldn't. How could he come back after running away the night before your wedding? He couldn't, could he?"

Molly froze, feeling Dorie's hand clutching hers and seeing the indignation in her eyes. That was probably what she should feel, too, but instead it was like the time she'd fallen from the apple tree and landed flat on her stomach— the breath knocked out of her so hard that she couldn't even gasp.

Chapter Three

It took a moment before Molly could catch her breath. She inhaled slowly, reminding herself to be calm. She didn't even know the tale was true. It might just be wishful thinking on Sally's part. And, anyway, what difference did it make?

The other children passed her, and most of them eyeing her with curiosity. Molly knew Aaron was standing close enough that he couldn't have missed hearing Dorie's announcement. She managed not to look at him, but she was very aware of his nearness and his gaze on her. No doubt, he was as curious as the kinder. But he was the very last person she'd want to explain her broken engagement to.

She pulled Dorie close to her as the last of the older scholars went by, ready to clap her hand over her sister's mouth to avoid any more indiscretions. At last, the schoolroom was empty except for them, and she took Dorie by the shoulders, looking down into her face…apprehensive now.

"Dorie, I'm ashamed of you. What would Mammi say if she heard you speak so about another member of the Leit?"

"But, Molly…"

"No buts about it. You go outside right now, and don't say a word to anyone. I'll be with you in a moment. Remember—no talking about William or his family."

Abashed at Molly's tone, Dorie blushed and scurried out the door, where Molly surely did hope she'd mind her tongue. No time to think about it… Teacher Grace was here already.

"Here is Aaron Fisher," Molly said quickly. No need to explain; the news of Aaron's arrival would have flashed around the Amish community in no time flat. "He wants to talk to you about his little girl, Becky. I'll just wait outside," she added, and went out the door nearly as fast as Dorie had.

That had probably been rude, but she couldn't seem to think straight just now. Besides, Aaron would want to talk to the teacher about Becky without her presence. He'd think what he had to say was none of her business, which it wasn't.

She hesitated on the small front porch, taking a deep breath of the autumn-scented air. The seasons changed whether folks were ready or not. Even the leaves showed just the smallest hint of the changes that were coming… changes that would bring visitors to enjoy the autumn colors, stare at the Amish people and fill up the inn.

Dorie stood by the picnic table under the spreading branches of an oak tree that had been there for longer than the schoolhouse had stood. Her hands were clasped in front of her, and her expression wavered between shame and defiance. When Molly started toward her, she settled on embarrassment, a flush rising from her neck to her cheeks so that they echoed the red of her hair.

"I'm sorry," Dorie burst out. "I shouldn't have said anything, I know. But I thought you'd feel so bad." Tears welled in her eyes, and Molly found her own heart wrenched.

"All right." Molly drew her little sister against her, feeling Dorie's body shake with the sobs she tried to hold back. "We'll forget it. But you must make up with Sally, yah?"

"I will. Right away." Dorie brushed the back of her hands across her eyes, and then she hesitated, looking at her big sister. "Are you okay? You don't…well, feel bad about William anymore?"

Molly patted her shoulder, not sure what to say. How much could a child Dorie's age understand of that combination of pain and embarrassment? She glanced at David, who loitered uncomfortably just out of earshot. He'd probably rather be with the boys playing kickball in the field, but true to the link between the twins, he waited. Even Lida, who was in a cluster of giggling girls, glanced over at them frequently.

But Dorie was waiting for an answer, and she had to find one. She focused on her little sister's face. "I've been too busy even to think about William lately. So, yah, I'm okay. Maybe just feel a little funny about seeing him."

"Maybe he won't come." Dorie's face brightened. "Sally might be wrong. She is, lots of times. And that's not saying anything bad about her," she added quickly. "Honest. Teacher Grace says sometimes her imagination needs to quiet down."

Molly had to repress a smile. That was probably true enough. Sally was known for telling tall stories. She patted Dorie's cheek.

"Well, time will tell. And if William does come back, it will make his family happy." She took a deep breath. "And it won't trouble me."

She spoke firmly, and hoped she sounded that way to her sister. The truth was that she didn't know what she'd feel if she saw William again, but she certain sure didn't want to talk to Dorie about it. Or anyone else.

The door to the schoolhouse opened, and Teacher Grace stepped out, followed by Aaron. Molly's nerves tightened, and she patted Dorie's cheek. "You run off now and make up with Sally. All right?"

Dorie nodded, twirled around and dashed off across the playground, clearly relieved at getting out of a situation she didn't understand.

Molly watched her for a moment, hoping she'd handled it the way Mammi would have. She saw Dorie hurry up to Sally, saw their exchange of words. Then the two of them raced off to the swings, holding hands.

"Ready to go?"

Aaron's deep voice didn't give a hint as to what his re-action was to the school, and his face didn't give anything away. She'd probably have to do some pushing to find out if she wanted to know.

Meanwhile she smiled, saying goodbye to Teacher Grace, and led the way back toward the path. Behind them, Molly could hear Teacher Grace's bell calling the scholars back to their studies.

They reached the lane, and Aaron was still silent. Molly brushed a graceful clump of Queen Anne's lace with her fingertips. "It's always fun for me to visit the school again. Not my brother. I think he's afraid Teacher Grace will ask if he's done his homework if he shows up here."

Aaron's lips moved slightly in what might have been meant for a smile. "She didn't seem very intimidating to me."

"You must have been a scholar who always did his homework," she said, hoping he might respond about his own school days.

He shrugged. "Too long ago to remember."

She opened her mouth to dispute that, then closed it again. Getting an unguarded word out of him was a chore, and she wondered if it was worthwhile. But she'd promised Leah she'd try her best to help.

"I'm sure Teacher Grace will be gentle with Becky."

He looked a bit startled. Did he really expect her to walk all the way back without mentioning the reason they'd come? Or was he too preoccupied with wondering about what Dorie had revealed?

Aaron shook his head. "Sorry. I was just wondering if Becky would settle all right." He seemed to try to include her, glancing at her face. "Yah, I'm sure you're right. From what I could see, Teacher Grace has a gift with the young ones."

"That she does." Molly's smile blossomed. "I'm sure she'd do everything possible to ease the transition for Becky. And with Dorie eager to be her friend—"

She stopped abruptly, realizing she'd run right into the subject she didn't want to talk about.

"Dorie seems to be a very friendly child," he said, his tone neutral.

"Friendly," Molly repeated. "Also outspoken, mischievous and a blabbermaul. She means well, but she never thinks before she speaks."

Aaron stopped, putting a hand on her wrist to stop her as well. "It's none of my business. You don't need to tell me anything."

She studied his face. He seemed to mean it. He really didn't care whether she told him or not. Quite suddenly, she realized that made it easy to blurt it out. After all, why not? If he didn't hear it from her, he'd hear it from someone else quick enough.

"What Dorie said was true. Two years ago, I was going to be married to Will Byler. The night before the wedding, he ran off, and I haven't heard from him since."

Why, she asked herself as she always did when she thought of it. *Why, Will?* How could she ever move on when she didn't know?

Aaron walked on automatically, reaching out now and then to hold a bramble away from Molly's dress. He couldn't think of a thing to say. How did Molly expect him to react?

He slid a glance sidelong at her face. She didn't look upset, exactly. But the atmosphere wasn't easy, either. He probably should apologize, but for what? It wasn't his doing that Molly's sister had blurted it out in front of him.

His irritability began to build. Aunt Leah should have told him this, so he'd be prepared. So he wouldn't stumble into saying the wrong thing.

Had he? His thoughts skittered back over their exchanges of the past day and didn't come up with anything, but maybe he should apologize in case he had.

Clearing his throat, he tried to find the words, but anything he said could make things worse. Finally, the words just stumbled out, like seed from a packet. "Molly, if I said anything that seemed like I was referring to that, I promise you that it didn't. I really didn't know anything about you and William." Well, that didn't seem very coherent. "Aunt Leah should have told me." The words burst out, exasperated.

"Ach, don't take on so, Aaron." Her words sounded almost genuine. "Goodness, in all the excitement of your arrival, and especially the joy of having Becky here, it's a wonder she remembered her own name."

She couldn't have said anything that would have gone through his defenses more quickly than that. "She really was happy, wasn't she? I've prayed their being together would be good for both of them."

"I'm sure it will." Her voice was warm. "Your aunt is good for people, and I sure enough have reason to know it. I couldn't have gotten through the last two years without out her kindness."

Aaron didn't want to hear about the disappointment of her wedding-that-wasn't, but he figured there was no way of avoiding it. She saw his face and chuckled, surprising him.

"Ach, don't worry. I'm not going to bore you with the details of what happened." Her face twitched. "All those presents to return, all the people who wanted to say they were sorry—ach, well, Leah was right there in the middle of it...packing up things to return them, helping Mammi give away all that food we'd prepared. She was a wonder, so calm and not blaming anyone."

"Yah, I can see that," he said softly, thinking about all the times when his aunt and uncle had come to help them with one crisis or another. Aunt Leah had been a wonder, all right.

Right up until his daad managed to explode some little thing into a big fight with his uncle. He had no doubts about who was to blame in that instance. His father always had a knack for taking things wrong. He hoped he hadn't inherited that.

They walked a little farther without speaking, and his mind was occupied with the past. Finally, he shook himself free.

"You said you owed Aunt Leah for getting you through those times, but it seems to me she benefited as much as you did. You learned the business so well that you've been running it yourself since her accident and taking care of her as well, ain't so?"

Rosy color came up in her cheeks. "Ach, it's not all on me. Everyone has been helping. They want to do it. Your aunt has done good for so many people here, whatever their trouble. You needn't think it was all me."

"Even so…" The concern came up in him again, and he pushed on doggedly. "You must have expected after all you've done that you wouldn't be forgotten when it came time for Aunt Leah to give up her property."

"Please, Aaron." Molly stopped in her tracks. "You mustn't think that. I never did. We all know how Leah felt about family."

"You've been as good as family to her. Better," he said stubbornly.

She was shaking her head. "I didn't expect anything. I still don't. I just want to do my job. You don't owe me anything. Except my salary, that is." Laughing, she turned, cutting through the brush to the farmyard behind the inn.

Aaron watched her, feeling as if she'd won that round. Except that they weren't fighting a battle, were they? Her slender figure moved through the grass, and she bent gracefully to pat the brown and white beagle that rose, tail wagging, from its nap on the porch of the inn.

She baffled him, and he didn't know why. And he had a feeling that he wasn't going to figure it out very easily.

Fortunately, Molly didn't have much time to think about Will's possible return or anything else that afternoon. No sooner than they'd finished cleaning up from lunch than she heard the sound of a car pulling into the parking lot. Leaning across the sink, she recognized the white van belonging to Tim Considine, the physical therapist who'd been assigned to work with Leah.

Brushing off her apron and checking that her kapp was tidy, Molly hurried to the back door to greet him. By then, Tim was pushing a wheelchair toward the porch.

Good, it looked as if Leah was to be allowed up at last. Leah's doctor had been very cautious during her recovery, talking about various dangers involved for a woman her age. Leah had reacted by calling him an old fuddy-duddy, which made him laugh. They were old friends, and despite arguing with him, Leah had the greatest respect for Doctor Chuck, as she called Dr. Wainwright .

Molly smiled, waving as Tim approached with his burden. Tim, with his curly brown hair and laughing brown eyes, was a familiar figure in Lost Creek, doing most of the home visits for therapy.

"Hello, wilkom! We didn't expect you today." She went down the two steps to help lift the chair up. They'd have to do something about a ramp soon. Several of the men had already volunteered to build it, so it wouldn't take long.

"Dr. Wainwright called the office and did some shoving. He wanted me here today, and you know he usually gets what he wants."

She laughed, nodding, and they maneuvered the chair through the door. "That probably means Leah had been shoving him. I know she wants to get out of that bed."

"Molly?" She turned to find Aaron regarding them from across the kitchen. He didn't look especially pleased to see her chattering about his aunt with a stranger.

She hurried to explain. "Aaron, this is Tim Considine, the physical therapist who is working with your aunt. Tim, did Leah mention her nephew to you? This is Aaron Fisher."

"She sure did mention that her nephew and his little girl were coming to stay. I'm sure she's excited to have you here." Aaron's only response was a nod, and Tim went on quickly. "Well, let's show Leah her new transport, okay?" He seemed to wait for someone to take the initiative.

Molly and Aaron both moved to open the door and collided in the doorway. "You don't need to come in. I'm sure you have other things to do." Aaron was frowning, and she wasn't sure why. Just being bossy?

"If I have to help her, I need to know how," she retorted. They glared at each other.

"You both need to know," Tim said, pushing the chair forward and forcing them to move on into Leah's room. "Let's get going."

The next hour was trying for everyone, and probably most of all for Aaron. He was clearly unused to caring for an injured person and seemed to be all thumbs, afraid of hurting his aunt by an unwary touch.

Leah was cautious, obviously eager to be mobile, but also fearful of doing the wrong thing, and she tended to cling to Molly, which didn't make Aaron happy. Molly realized that it was a situation where Leah wanted a woman, and someone familiar to her, but she couldn't very well explain at the moment. Maybe later there'd be an opportunity.

Fortunately, there was an interruption before anyone's frayed nerves snapped. Noises and chatter were heard in the kitchen, and a moment later someone rushed the bedroom door. Molly knew who it was immediately, and was prepared when Dorie burst in.

Aaron looked ready to scold, but Leah smiled. "Look at me, Dorie. I can move myself." She demonstrated, pushing the wheels with her hands.

Dorie's "Wow!" was quickly drowned out by other comments as David and Mammi came in behind her. Mammi grabbed Dorie before she could attempt to climb onto the chair. "Leah, this is wonderful news. You are getting better for sure."

Leah clung to Mammi's hand, and Molly saw her eyes glaze with tears. "Yah, at last. Denke." Heads close together, Leah and Mammi exchanged a few whispered words no one else could hear.

Old friends, Molly thought. They had the sort of deep women's friendship that spoke of joys and sorrows shared over many years. She blinked back tears of her own.

Molly noticed that Aaron was still frowning, probably thinking there were a lot of people and noise in the room. But she could see the pleasure in Leah's face and knew how isolated she'd been feeling. This could only be good for her.

She was about to say something reassuring, but Mammi beat her to it. Standing, still holding Leah's hand, Mammi smiled at Aaron. "We're a noisy bunch, ain't so? It's because we're all happy to see your aunt doing better. I'm Molly's mother, and you're Aaron. I remember you from when you were a little boy."

Aaron looked a little overwhelmed, as if not sure what to respond to first. Mammi's outgoing, overflowing affection sometimes had that effect on people who didn't know her.

Mammi turned back to Leah. "I brought the twins with me so they can get acquainted with Becky before she starts school. They'll go home with Molly when it's time to leave."

Seeing his confusion, Molly spoke quickly to Aaron.

"My mother is staying tonight, that's what's going on. But I didn't know the twins were coming. I'll go find Becky."

She slid out of the room, not surprised to find David coming along with her. Dorie had gotten all of the outgoing nature of the twins, while he preferred to hang back and let her carry the ball.

"Too many people in there, right?" She grinned at him as they went up the stairs.

He nodded, mumbling that he was glad Leah was better. They reached the top, and he looked around wide-eyed. "She has the room with the secret closet?" All the children had been here often enough to know about it. When Molly nodded, he had another question. "Can I see?"

Every child introduced to the secret seemed to have the same fascination. Molly took his hand. "Komm. We'll ask Becky."

Becky was curled up on the window seat with a book. Her face lit when she saw Molly and then stiffened as David came in. Molly pretended not to notice. "Here is David, and Dorie is downstairs. They wanted to wilkom you since you'll be in their grade at school."

Becky slid off the seat, smoothing down her skirt. She said hello so softly that David probably didn't hear it. Likely the two of them would have trouble carrying on a conversation since neither of them would take the lead. However, she could be sure that Dorie wouldn't let anything hold her back.

David pulled at her sleeve. "Ask her about the secret closet," he whispered.

"Right. David wants to see the closet, Becky. Would you show it to him?"

Becky gave him a shy smile and led the way to the closet,

seeming to take pride in showing him the secret of the latch. They both popped their heads inside, and she heard a few words exchanged between them. Good, she wouldn't have to speak for both of them.

At that moment, Dorie called from downstairs. "Molly? Where are you?"

"We're just coming down," she said, thinking it would be a good idea to get all the kids outside so Mamm and Leah could have time together. "We'll go pick some things in the garden."

Dorie's response was typical. "Do we have to?"

"Yah, you do." Collecting David and Becky, she headed downstairs. Giving them a chore to do together would break the ice better than anything.

When they reached the kitchen, Mammi was pushing Leah's wheelchair up to the table. "We'll just have tea and some of the cookies I brought."

David looked up at the mention of cookies, and Mammi shook her head, smiling. "You young ones go on outside with Molly. You can have yours on the porch later."

"That's right." Molly took a basket from the hook by the door. "Come along now."

The children scurried after her, and to her surprise, Aaron came with them. He paused by the door, glancing back at his aunt, and then followed her.

Molly gave Aaron a reassuring smile as they went down the steps together. "Mamm will look after her. She'll be fine."

Aaron blinked. "I'm sure. They've been friends for a long time, yah?"

"Since they were girls together," she answered, wondering what was on Aaron's mind.

"It's easy to see." His face relaxed suddenly, as if something had reassured him. "They're a lot alike."

Molly went off to get the kinder started in the garden, which had been sadly neglected since Leah's accident, but she turned his words over in her mind. It seemed to her that he was making a quick judgment about both of them. They had years of friendship in common, yah, but their personalities were different in many ways.

Both of them would go a long way to help others, that was certain sure. But while their generosity wasn't in question, she'd always thought that Leah was prone to decide what was best for others and push them in that direction, as she had with Molly.

That was fine when it was right, but what if it wasn't the path the other person would choose? She had accepted Leah's plan for her gratefully, knowing it was just what she needed at the time, but what about Aaron? She suspected he also had a mind of his own, and his aunt might find it not so easy to direct him the way she wanted.

"Is this one the right size?" David held up a very large zucchini that Molly looked at in dismay. The garden had definitely gotten away from them.

"What's wrong, Molly? Don't you like them the size of a baseball bat?" Aaron spoke from behind her, surprising a giggle out of her.

"I think it might be a little big for what I have in mind. Can you help the others find some about a third that size?"

David seemed to measure it visually, and then he nodded. "What do you want me to do with this one?"

"I'll take it." Aaron held out his hand.

"Denke." He tossed it to Aaron as he would to his older brother, then looked apprehensive.

But Aaron caught it easily. "Compost is behind the barn, right?"

She nodded. "Yah, and you don't need to tell me that the garden got away from us."

"Not surprising after Aunt Leah's accident." His thoughts seemed to be elsewhere. "I'm thinking that tomorrow we need to get together and make plans for the guests who are coming on Saturday."

She opened her mouth to suggest they go ahead as they always did, and then closed it again. What had she just been telling herself?

Leah would probably want to run things the way she always had. Aaron had ideas of his own. Right or wrong, she suspected there were going to be clashes in the future. And she would probably be right in the middle.

Chapter Four

❦

"You'd best stop wiggling," Molly said, laughing. "Or I can't guarantee your hair will stay under your kapp."

Becky giggled, and Molly's heart swelled with thanksgiving. How wonderful good it was to hear her sounding like a normal eight-year-old, even if it only lasted a few minutes.

"Now, let's put an extra pin or two in to hold it." She smoothed the child's soft yellow hair, making sure the kapp sat securely in place.

"Does Dorie have an extra pin in her hair?"

She wasn't surprised to find Becky wanting to copy Dorie. Their hour together had produced good results, one of which was Becky's determination to start school today. Aaron had been hesitant, thinking she should wait until Monday, but Leah and Molly had combined to persuade him to let her go today, since she was so enthusiastic.

"Yah, at least one extra one," she told Becky. "Dorie runs around so much at recess that Mammi says nothing but staples could hold her hair under her kapp."

Becky giggled again, started toward her bedroom door and then looked back at Molly, a little apprehension showing. "Will I…" She hesitated, and then went on. "Will I be able to sit next to Dorie?" A cloud crossed her face. "Will she want me to?"

"For sure, she will." Molly enveloped her in a quick hug. "And Teacher Grace will say it's all right."

In fact, Grace had already said she'd seat Becky next to Dorie and right in front of David. Molly had made sure of it last night, but it hadn't been necessary. Teacher Grace wouldn't forget anything to make her new scholar feel at home.

They walked downstairs hand in hand to find Aunt Leah waiting with Aaron in the kitchen.

"Becky, you look just right," Leah exclaimed. "Doesn't she, Aaron?"

Aaron had been looking at Molly with a slight frown, but he quickly switched to a warm smile for Becky. "Just right," he echoed, and he held out his hand to his daughter. "You're going to do fine."

Becky's smile was a little uncertain, but she took the lunch bag Molly held out to her and grasped her father's hand.

"We'll be waiting to hear all about it when you get home," Molly said, hoping she was saying what the child wanted to hear.

Becky's answering smile seemed to say she'd guessed right. *Let it be a good day for her. Please.* She said the words silently in her heart and walked to the door to wave goodbye. They'd meet her siblings at the point where the path led up to the school. But probably Aaron would stay with Becky until she was in the classroom and settled.

As they went down the steps, Aaron glanced back at her. "I won't be gone long. When I get back, we can have that talk."

Molly nodded, managing to hold onto her smile. She'd been thinking about Aaron's hints of making changes, and wondering what Leah's reactions would be. Leah might think she was ready to let go of the reins, but actually doing it might be a different thing.

When she stepped back inside, it was clear that Leah had heard. That didn't mean she'd ask about it, Molly told herself, taking dishes to the sink. "I'll get going on the dishes unless you need something," she said quickly.

"Let them wait a bit and have some more coffee," Leah said firmly. "What does Aaron need to talk to you about?"

Here it was already, and she really didn't want to get between Leah and her nephew. Of course, maybe there wouldn't be any disagreement. Or maybe Leah meant it that she was putting the inn into Aaron's hands. In any event, Molly had to say something. She poured coffee to give herself a moment.

Leah raised her eyebrows, looking impatient. Somehow, the fact that she was upright and sitting in the wheelchair had made her more interested in what was going on. That was good, for sure. Much better than those days when she lay in bed, not moving, barely responding.

"Well?"

"Don't be so impatient," she teased, smiling. "I think he wants to go over the plans for our visitors on the weekend."

"Yah, I'd forgotten this is the weekend the Bradfords are coming. And that new couple that are friends of theirs."

Mr. and Mrs. Bradford were regular visitors, coming several times in the fall to follow the progression of the season. This time they'd invited another couple to join them. That meant they'd be eager to have everything just right.

"Yah, they confirmed a few days ago. Arriving late afternoon on Friday and leaving Sunday afternoon."

"Just like usual." She nodded decisively. "Good people for the first time Aaron is running things. All he needs to do is let you take care of it, like you always do."

"Well…"

"Well, what?" Leah's fingers tightened around her coffee spoon, the veins standing out on the back of her hand.

Molly tried to look assured but feared her smile was questioning. "Nothing. But it's possible he'll want to make some changes now that he's in charge, ain't so?"

"Changes?" Leah's voice went up, and Molly steadied herself.

"Well, that would be natural, wouldn't it? People always want to make some changes when they take charge. That's the normal thing to do."

Leah hesitated a few minutes before nodding. "I guess so."

Molly had thought about it, but she hadn't come up with any answers. Daad would say she should stay out of it, but she couldn't. She just wasn't made that way.

Leah studied her face for a long moment. Then she shook her head, her expression tightening. "You don't make changes until you know what's what. Aaron will know that."

"But…" Molly let her voice die away. She'd been trying to help, and she'd only made matters worse. She started again. "I just thought it was possible. But I'm sure you're right."

Her ears caught the welcome sound of a buggy coming up the driveway. "Someone's here." Molly stood, putting her coffee cup in the sink. Whoever it was had picked a good time to interrupt.

Leah's chair was nearer the screen door, so she identified the driver before Molly had a chance to. Then she turned toward Molly as she backed her chair away from the door.

"It must be for you. It's Will Byler's mother."

Molly's breath caught. This morning had been difficult enough as it was. Now she'd have to find a way to cope with Sarah Byler. Why would she come calling on her now?

Unless, of course, that tale about Will coming home was true.

Aaron walked back along the lane. The trip to the schoolhouse had taken longer than he'd expected, but he didn't hurry. It was a beautiful morning, with just a hint of autumn's coolness in the air, and his heart felt lighter than it had in a long time.

After all the worrying he'd done about how Becky would react to school, she'd slipped into place as if she'd always been there. Teacher Grace had encouraged him to stay and observe for a time, saying that he'd want to be sure Becky felt safe and happy.

Teacher Grace knew far more about their situation than he'd expected, but of course she would. Between them, Aunt Leah and Molly would have passed on everything they knew and plenty they'd probably imagined.

He slowed, picking a faded blossom from a clump of Queen Anne's lace and letting it crumble in his fingers, where it left a faint pleasant smell. He shouldn't be thinking that of Aunt Leah, after all her kindness to him. Or about Molly, for that matter. He didn't know her well enough to accuse her of being a blabbermaul, and he had to be fair.

Still, she made him feel uncomfortable… Why? Not because of anything she'd said. No, it was his sense that he was taking away something she'd expected to be hers. She hadn't said anything to indicate she felt that way, but how could she help it? She'd done far more than he had to help, that was certain sure.

That fact should make him feel grateful to her, instead of having this mix of blame and self-consciousness that made him say the wrong thing at every opportunity.

Well, he'd just have to try harder. He dusted the last fragments of flower from his hand and headed up the path toward the barn. As he came into the open, Aaron caught sight of a buggy disappearing onto the main road. Early company, it seemed. He hurried his steps toward the house.

When Aaron walked into the kitchen, Aunt Leah was sitting at the kitchen table, coffee cup in hand. She greeted him with a smile.

"All is well at the school, ain't so?"

"Yah, Becky settled down right away." He should say something grateful about Molly's brother and sister. He looked at Molly, but she stood at the sink, her back to him, not looking around. He turned back to his aunt.

"She made friends with Teacher Grace right away. And Dorie and David were wonderful good to her."

He thought Molly's back stiffened a bit. Then she was scooting to the cellar door, still without looking. She muttered something about the laundry and vanished.

Aaron swung back to his aunt. "What's the matter with her? All I did was say something nice about the twins."

Aunt Leah shook her head, and her gaze was disapproving. "It's nothing to do with you." She hesitated, as if not sure she should confide in him, but then went on. "Will Byler's mother was just here to see her. I think it upset her."

"Oh." He couldn't help but wonder about that. "Is she...

Molly…on good terms with them?" He wanted to bite his tongue. Of all the things that weren't his business, that was at the top of the list. "It's not curiosity," he added hastily. "I just don't want to say the wrong thing."

"Molly doesn't blame them for anything. They were heartbroken when Will left. But I don't know what Sarah Byler wanted today." Concern was written on her face. "All I know is that Molly has been upset since she came. So just don't mention it to her."

"Yah, sure. I'll be careful." How careful did he have to be? Could he go ahead and talk to Molly about the plans for the weekend? That was business, not personal.

Aunt Leah seemed to think she'd said enough, or maybe too much. She murmured something about finding her knitting and wheeled herself toward the living room.

Aaron stood there, undecided, for a moment. Then he heard Molly coming up the stairs from the cellar. *Business*, he reminded himself. They'd best get on with it.

He was waiting when she emerged, carrying a quart jar in each hand. "Is that for supper?" He nodded toward the jars.

"What?" Molly looked as if she didn't know what he was talking about. Then she glanced at the jars. "Oh, no. Your aunt thought this vegetable soup would be good for lunch."

He glanced at the clock. "Looks like we have time to talk about the weekend before lunchtime. Let's go over to the office." Starting toward the other part of the house, he heard first silence behind him. Then her footsteps sounded.

The office was a small room next to the side door of the inn, close to the parking lot. Just enough room for a desk, a filing cabinet, a calendar showing bookings, several racks on the wall holding keys to the various rooms and a computer and printer.

He glanced at Molly, sensing the tension that held her rigid.

"I'll have to leave the computer to you." He tried to sound as if he didn't notice the strain that deepened the slight creases in her forehead.

"What? Oh, yah, that's fine. The community agrees that you can't run a business without using a computer, but I'm the only one at the inn who's learned how." Her slight smile wavered. "And I promise you, I don't use it for anything but business."

"I'm sure of that. I didn't mean to sound critical."

She shrugged. "You didn't. But other communities have agreed to different rules about it, and I didn't know about yours."

"Probably about the same." He moved to the desk, and she stepped aside to give him space. "Maybe you could show me the reservations book, so I know what's coming up."

Molly reached across the desk, her sleeve brushing his. She grabbed a ledger and flipped it open, smoothing the page flat. "Here's the list of upcoming weeks. You'll see there are just a few weekends booked for this month, but then it gets very busy."

He reached across to turn the page, and their hands touched as she did the same. For an instant, they both froze. The small room seemed to close in on them. Aaron drew back, scolding himself.

He had no reason to feel anything at all for Molly, especially that oddly breathless feeling he couldn't explain. Molly stared at her hand, as if not sure it was hers.

"Sorry." He tried to laugh. "There's not much room in here."

"No. Usually I'm the only one working here." Her lips formed a smile that didn't reach her eyes. To his horror, he saw them fill with tears.

"I'm sorry," he said again. He spoke without taking thought, just letting the words come. "I shouldn't have suggested doing this now. I could see you were upset."

She wiped her eyes with her fingers. "Sorry. That's foolish of me." A flush mounted to her cheeks, deepening her color. "We… I had a visitor while you were out."

Aunt Leah had said not to mention it, but what could he do when Molly brought it up?

"Yah, I saw the buggy leaving. Aunt Leah…" He stopped. Bad enough he'd ignored his aunt's advice. At least he shouldn't lay any blame on her.

"It's all right." Her lips curved softly, but again tears filled her eyes. He wanted to reach out to her, but he knew he shouldn't. She wouldn't welcome it.

"Everyone will know soon, so I'd best get used to it. It sounds like Will is coming home. His mother said she had a letter from him. He wanted her to ask if it was all right with me."

It sounded to him as if the unknown Will was trying to salve his own conscience by putting the burden on her. Or maybe trying to ensure that no one would make his return difficult. But Aaron couldn't very well say that.

"So you said it was fine, because you didn't want to hurt her feelings," he predicted. Again, he felt a surge of annoyance toward the man.

A tear spilled over onto her cheek, and without thought,

he brushed it away with his fingertip. Then he drew back as if he'd been stung.

"Sorry," he said quickly. "Look, we don't have to do this now." He nodded toward the ledger. "You just tell me when we can talk about it. I'll…" He gestured toward the door. "I'll find something else to do."

Aaron strode quickly to the hallway and then through the door that led onto the porch. He'd just said and done all the things he shouldn't have. And, somehow, he didn't regret it.

Stepping off the porch, he headed toward the barn. There was always something to do there. A little physical labor was the best way to chase these thoughts from his mind.

In the small powder room, Molly splashed some cold water on her face, tried to smile, and then dismissed the expression as ineffective. She'd certainly made a fool of herself by breaking down in front of Aaron. She'd told herself she had no feelings left for Will, but if so, why did she react that way? Just saying it out loud to Aaron seemed to bring it home to her.

Aaron probably thought she'd been begging for sympathy. Or trying to get out of making plans with him. She should have had more control of herself. Why had she opened up to Aaron that way? Neither of them wanted it.

She smoothed down the white apron she wore over her favorite blue dress. Leah had insisted that since she would be working more with visitors to the inn, she should have a couple of new dresses for the fall. It hadn't taken much to talk her into it, but Leah had also insisted on paying for the fabric, no matter how Molly argued. She'd probably still be trying to give it back if Mamm hadn't told her to look at it like a waitress's uniform.

The blue was lovely, and she'd begun work on the green one last night. She started up the stairs to the guest rooms, glad to find that thinking about clothes had been enough to distract her. She made a note to put more tissues in the bathrooms and pillowcases in the upstairs linen closet before she headed back downstairs.

A few more simple chores with no one talking to her had Molly feeling almost normal. She shoved all thoughts about Will to the back of her mind to consider later. Right now, she'd best have that talk with Aaron about plans for the weekend. Picking up the red notebook she used for her daily to-do list, she went in search of Aaron.

She found him on the back porch, oiling the hinges on the swing. It was on the tip of her tongue to warn him not to get oil on the cushions, but decided in time that wouldn't be tactful.

"If you have a few minutes, maybe you'd like to run over the plans for the weekend."

The screen door shut behind her, and Aaron swung around. She noticed again how sturdy and broad-shouldered he was. It was easy to imagine him working on construction. She wouldn't think he'd find this work congenial, but she knew determination when she saw it. He'd do whatever it took to give his child a good future.

Molly gestured with the notebook. "I thought you might want to take a few minutes to talk about plans for the weekend. If you have time, that is."

He leaned to one side so that he could see through the screen to the kitchen clock. "Yah, I have some time before I need to go pick up Becky." He gave her a cautious look. "Sure you're up to it?"

"Yah, of course." She managed to smile. "I have all my notes here."

"Komm, sit down." He gestured to the swing. "You can see if that stops all the creaking it's doing."

She sat on the cushioned swing and pushed cautiously with one foot. The tiniest creak sounded. "Just right," she said quickly, before he could reach for the oilcan again. "It wouldn't feel like a porch swing if it didn't have a little squeak when it's pushed."

Aaron shrugged, sitting down in the rocking chair on the other side of a small table. "Okay, fine. Aunt Leah told me about the one couple who've been here before. That's gut."

"They are nice folks, and they really seem to enjoy it here." She glanced at the surrounding woods. "More so when the leaves are turning."

He nodded. "It won't be that long. Aunt Leah says that you and Hilda can take care of the rooms and so forth. But I wondered about breakfast."

"I can manage that, I'm certain sure. We do fresh fruit, juice, a breakfast casserole, cereal, bacon and sausage, breads…"

He was frowning, and she let her voice trail away.

"I'm thinking these Englischh people might want something they're used to. If we gave them a menu to order from, they'd maybe like that better. You wouldn't waste so much food that way, ain't so?"

Molly had a quick negative response, and she hoped her face didn't give her away. "Guests seem to like what we serve." *Why do you want to change it when you haven't even tried it?*

She managed not to say it out loud.

"Maybe they'll like this better." He sounded impatient. "You can do it, can't you…cooking it to order?"

She nodded. What did he think she did every day?

"Gut." He gave a short nod. "Make up a simple menu, and we can get some copies made before the weekend."

It sounded as if what she thought wasn't under consideration. She couldn't argue about it, not after what Leah had said. But she couldn't just let it go, either.

She stared at the worn floorboards of the porch as she rocked gently, trying to think of how to put it.

"I'm not sure changes are a good thing. Especially with people who've been here before. They might not expect it."

Aaron's face tightened. "That's the whole point of changes—to give people something new."

"Yah, but…maybe it would be a gut idea to run it by your aunt?" She made it a question rather than a statement.

That didn't seem to help. His expression grew so stiff it looked like it was carved out of stone. He stood up abruptly. "If that's what it takes to persuade you to do what I tell you…"

"No, of course not," she said hurriedly. "I just thought…" Once again, she let the sentence die away. She seemed to do that a lot with Aaron. She shook her head. "Is there anything else you want to change for the weekend?"

"I notice there aren't any notepads in the bedrooms. Maybe you can pick some up when you get the groceries next time."

It sounded like a suggestion, but she knew it wasn't one. "Yah, sure. Anything else?"

For a moment, his expression softened, and it seemed he'd say something. But then he shook his head. "That's all for now." He turned to look at the clock through the screen.

"I should get moving to pick Becky up at school." His lips clamped shut, and he stepped off the porch.

Molly sat still for a moment. She didn't like it, but her instinct told her not to take it to Leah. She wasn't going to become a buffer between them. It wasn't going to be easy to prevent it, but she'd have to try.

Shaking her head, Molly went back into the kitchen. It was time she got an after-school snack ready for Becky, and she'd check on Leah. Leah would certain sure want to be ready to hear about Becky's first day.

By the time Molly spotted Becky swinging on her father's hand as she came down the path, Leah was settled at the table with coffee and one of Molly's snickerdoodle cookies. Molly set a pitcher of lemonade on the table and put out glasses.

Still hanging onto her father's hand, Becky tugged him into the kitchen. Seeing her Aunt Leah and Molly waiting, her small face burst into a big smile. "It was such a gut day," she exclaimed. "Aunt Leah, I got to sit next to Dorie. And David is sitting right behind me. Isn't that nice?"

"It's wonderful gut." Leah drew the child close to her. "I'm so glad. That will make you feel at home, yah?"

"Yah. Molly, did you tell Teacher Grace to put them near me?"

Molly answered the smile, pouring out lemonade. "I didn't tell her," she said distinctly, wondering if Aaron would notice. But he seemed engrossed in getting himself coffee. "I asked her what she thought, and she said it was a good idea."

"Yah, it was. And we all played together at recess. And I shared my cookies with them. I love snickerdoodles and they do, too."

She nodded. "Who doesn't love snickerdoodles, yah?" She picked up the breakfast menu she'd been working on from the counter and handed it to Aaron.

Startled, he looked at it and then smiled, meeting her gaze. "That's fine, Molly. Denke."

She nodded and tried to look enthusiastic, but she didn't feel that way. Whether he was right or wrong, if Aaron continued to ignore her suggestions, she just might have to look for another job.

Chapter Five

It was all very well to decide she'd keep the peace by letting Aaron have his way, Molly decided, but over the next day or two, she was biting her lip so much it was getting sore.

"Here, grab that end." Hilda, on the other side of the double bed, was pulling up the clean sheet. "Are you half asleep this morning? Or just grumpy?"

"I'm not either of those," she said firmly. "Just thinking of something." She grabbed the end of the sheet, catching the fresh scent of the outdoors as she did. "Smells good. Leah says that's one of the things people always say they like here."

Hilda tucked it under, laughing a little. "It probably doesn't make them hang out their wash instead of using their electric dryers."

Molly nodded, smiling. She'd much rather talk about sheets dried on the line than think about Aaron's habit of telling her to do things that she already intended to do.

Hilda lifted a questioning eyebrow. "You can't fool me. I know when you're annoyed with someone. And I can figure out who it is, too."

"Hush." Molly darted a glance toward the door. "I don't know why I let myself get annoyed. After all, he's the boss now. It never bothered me before to do what I was told."

"Before what? You mean back when you were a meek little teenager?" Hilda shook her head. "You've changed since then—for one thing, you're not so shy about speaking your mind. That's a good thing."

"Is it good? I'm not so sure." Together they pulled up the double wedding ring quilt and smoothed it into place.

"Take it from an old married woman," Hilda said. "Plenty of men like women who can think for themselves. Jonah says it would be boring if we thought alike about everything."

Molly tossed a pillowcase to her. "You picked a prize when it came to husbands. Jonah is a sweetheart, everyone knows that."

"I'll tell him that the next time he disagrees with me," she said, laughing.

"You do that." Molly began stuffing a pillow into the pillowcase, wondering if what Hilda said was true. If it was, probably the blame...or the thanks...belonged to Will. His defection had turned her life upside down and inside out. Leah had helped, too, pushing her into situations where she had to deal with people and their problems and even tell others what to do.

And now Leah's nephew was trying her patience, to say nothing of her temper. Somehow, talking to Hilda helped, as it always had. If she was changing, as Hilda said, she'd just have to get used to it.

A floorboard creaked behind her, and she knew without looking that Aaron had arrived to check up on her. He greeted Hilda and prowled around the room, probably looking for something wrong.

"Didn't you say you were putting flowers in the rooms?"

She kept her voice calm and even. "That's right. I'll cut

the mums tomorrow morning, so they'll be fresh when the guests arrive."

He nodded, then switched to the bed covers. "Maybe we should put a blanket on the bed. Nights are getting chillier."

Chilly nights were nothing compared to what she was feeling. And on this topic, she had a good reason to tell him so. "It happens that this couple doesn't like an extra blanket on the bed. She told me the last time they were here that her husband was always throwing the extra covers off."

"And you remembered that?" He sounded doubtful.

"My memory isn't that good. But I made a note of it, so we'd remember this time. That was Leah's idea... She says it's an easy way to make people feel at home." Quoting Leah seemed to do the trick. Aaron just nodded and looked away.

Hilda flicked a duster across the dresser she'd already cleaned and winked at Molly. "I'll just go down and check on Leah."

Molly knew exactly what she was thinking. Hilda was getting out of the way and telling Molly to stand up to him. But whether Hilda was here or not, she was determined not to say another word about it. She made a face at Hilda and realized, too late, that Aaron had probably seen it.

She risked a glance at him to find that he apparently hadn't noticed. He was frowning, tracing one of the circles on the quilt. "This is a wedding ring quilt, right?"

That was a change of subject, for sure.

"A double wedding ring quilt, actually." She ran her finger around the double circles. "All the quilts for the guest rooms are handmade...some by Leah, some by my mamm or another woman in the community. Aunt Leah did this one."

"I can't imagine putting those pieces together. That must

be a gift," he said, seemingly distracted from his list of directions.

"Lots of practice, that's all. Mammi was determined I'd learn." Her mind slipped to the sunshine and shadows quilt she'd made for her wedding. That one ought to be just called shadows.

She shook the thought away and smiled. "I didn't know you were interested in quilting."

He shrugged. "I figured we'd better talk about something else, since I was driving you up the wally with everything I said."

Molly could feel the flush mounting to her cheeks as she struggled to hold onto her smile. "You didn't... I mean, I wasn't." She might as well have a fever, as hot as her skin felt.

"Sure I did." A smile teased at the corners of his mouth. When she responded, his smile spread, putting laughter lines around the corners of his eyes. "I'm sorry for hassling you. I guess the truth is that I'm nervous about the first guests when I'm here. I don't want to disappoint Aunt Leah."

Molly suddenly realized he meant it. Behind the stern look he often wore, his eyes betrayed him. Aaron was as nervous as a boy on his first date. She didn't know whether to laugh or cry. She'd been thinking Aaron had everything just the way he wanted it, but the other side of that was the awareness other people had to want it, too.

"I'd feel the same," she said, feeling as if she'd like to pat his shoulder and tell him everything would be all right, the way she would with the twins. "It's going to be fine. These people are pleasant and happy to be coming here. They won't be hard to please. Just do what you think your aunt would do."

"Easy enough for you to say. You've been around her enough to know." He took a deep breath, his chest moving. "Anyway, I'll try. I may not sound like it, but I really am glad to have you here working with me."

She ought to respond that she was glad to work with him, too, but she couldn't quite say it and sound convincing. "This weekend will be fine. Everything is set up, and I know they'll enjoy themselves."

A rumble of thunder seemed to punctuate her words, and she darted a look at the window. While she'd been working here, a mass of dark clouds had been moving in from the west.

"The laundry," she wailed. "I've got to get it off the line." She darted for the door and scurried down the steps, hearing Aaron's quick footsteps behind her. He surely didn't intend to help, did he? She felt quite sure he'd consider that women's work.

Whether he did or not, he beat her to the porch door, grabbed a basket, and headed for the clothesline. His response was something she certain sure hadn't anticipated.

Well, maybe she'd been wrong about his attitude, odd as it seemed, but she'd hate to count on it.

Bringing in laundry was one of the things Aaron had had to figure out after his wife died. Actually, it was one of the easiest, not that he'd had to do it all that often. Usually his mother took care of that sort of thing, but if his willingness to help favorably impressed Molly, so much the better.

He'd been trying to do that when he'd sought her out this morning, and then he'd messed it up even before he'd started. His apprehension over entertaining their first set of guests had spilled out, and she'd obviously thought he was criticizing her.

No, he'd best be honest with himself. He had been critical, and for no good reason. He had no right to take his sense of inadequacy out on Molly. The pillowcase he was folding developed creases when he clenched his fist. Shaking it out, he started again.

Molly had started at the other end of the line. Her movements were quick, yet efficient. She didn't waste energy. Every movement seemed to flow into the next one. He could do this for the next fifty years and never look like that.

"Looks like it's going to hold off long enough to get things in, at least." A rumble of thunder rolled across the valley, and lightning flickered.

Stepping a little closer to her, he started on the next sheet. "Do you have to do all the laundry? Seems like someone should help with this." Just because she made everything look easy, didn't mean it was.

"I have help. Hilda would have started it today, but she couldn't get here as early as usual." Molly's next step brought her closer to him. She cast another measuring look at the clouds. "Usually at this time of the year, the storms come later in the day."

He nodded in agreement, and they reached for the last sheet simultaneously. Molly laughed. "You take that side and I'll take the other."

A vivid lightning stroke cracked earthward, followed closely by a clap of thunder that seemed to deafen him for a moment.

"Best hurry." He shook the side he held as Molly did the same on the other. He followed her movements, straightening the side in his hands and then moving toward her to fold. His fingers brushed hers, and they seemed to tingle, as if the lightning had rippled along them.

Shaking off the idea, he moved back to catch the other end. It was as if they were involved in a dance, moving forward to meet and then backward again. Forward and backward... That was the process of learning to work with Molly. Close and then back again—he had to eliminate some of those backward steps. They were stuck in this situation, and they both needed it to succeed.

Did Molly feel the same? He glanced at her face, but she was focused on the chore in front of her.

Wind swept down the valley, the gusts flipping the leaves and sending loose twigs flying. Another crack of thunder seemed to roll across the sky, echoing from the hills. He took the sheet from her hands, stuffed it in the basket, and grabbed both the basket and Molly's hand.

"Move." He tugged her as they raced for the porch, feeling the first fat drops of rain hit them.

They ran up the steps and through the door, laughing and breathless as they came to a halt in the small mudroom. He saw her face, lit by laughter, as she looked up at him. For a moment, there were no differences between them.

"We made it," she said.

He nodded, taking a grasp on reality and dismissing distractions. "I don't mind getting wet myself, but I didn't want to ruin your laundry."

"Denke," she said, with a gesture almost like a bow. Perhaps she'd been thinking of a dance between them, too.

"Aaron, Molly, are you out there? What are you doing?" His aunt's voice chased away the last of the random thoughts.

"Coming in," he called, opening the door into the kitchen.

"Gut." Aunt Leah sat in the wheelchair pulled up to the

table. "I didn't want you to get soaked." A spray of water rattled the windowpanes, and she shivered a little.

"We're fine." He put his arm around Aunt Leah's shoulders while Molly stacked sheets on the closet shelves devoted to inn linens. "I just hope it stops before it's time for school to be out."

"It will," she assured him. "A sign of fall, I think."

He nodded. "Becky told me that Dorie is learning to make a quilt. She says Dorie said it's going to be big enough to put on her bed." His aunt chuckled, and Molly smiled.

"I'm afraid that's an example of Dorie's wishful thinking," Molly said, closing the closet door. "She wants it to be that big, but Mammi is starting off on a nine-patch quilt for her doll's bed."

"That's a good first step," Leah said. "Does that mean that Becky wants to make one, too?"

"Yah, it does." He rubbed the back of his neck, wishing he didn't have to ask for help with his child. "Molly mentioned that you made the quilt she was putting on the bed upstairs, so I hoped you might be able to teach her."

"The double wedding ring quilt?" She shot a look at Molly. "Seems like Dorie's not the only one to exaggerate."

The flush rose in Molly's cheeks again, making him want to smile. "Now, Leah, you know the planning and cutting was all yours."

"Yah, and I know I had to turn it over to you to finish because I was too busy. So you're the one who made it."

Molly just shook her head, smiling.

"Anyway, either or both of you…would you be able to teach her?" He frowned. "That's another of the things I can't do for her." Too many, he feared.

"For sure we will," Aunt Leah nodded, smiling. "But as

for that, maybe it's time you thought about giving Becky a stepmother."

Leah had spoken teasingly, but his face froze for a moment. That was the sort of thing that caught a person unaware, cutting through the layers of protection around the heart. He didn't answer... He couldn't.

Molly spoke quickly, filling in the moment. "I'll get out that box of fabric we have upstairs to see if there's anything she likes. And maybe Dorie could come over and they could work together sometimes."

"I'd forgotten about that box," Leah said, distracted. "Yah, let's look at that."

Aaron wanted to thank Molly for rescuing him, but he couldn't say the words. Still, he could see it wasn't necessary. Molly was good at jumping in to help people. And good as well at not holding a grudge. The better he got to know her, the more he thought William must have been a very foolish young man.

Molly had seen Aaron's reaction to his aunt's comment. Goodness knows what Leah had been thinking. For all her knowledge, Leah had made a mistake there. It was clear Aaron had never gotten over his wife's death. She imagined he'd never even considered such a thing as marrying again. Possibly someday, but not now.

And even if he had considered it, the whole business would be complicated. Becky was so sensitive... She wouldn't want to hear a comment like that, and if Leah meant it as a joke, Becky wouldn't understand.

Aaron murmured something about checking the barn roof for any leaks and hastened out the door before anything else could be said about marriage. Not looking at Leah,

Molly started a chicken stewing for potpie and mixed up the dough to make noodles. The rain was slacking off, and even as she thought it, the sun peeked through.

"Typical September weather here," Leah said, moving her chair over to the table. "Hand me that dough when it's ready to be rolled out. No reason I can't do that here." She smacked her palm down on the table.

Molly bit back any argument. If it was too much for Leah, she should be able to tell, and doing something would be better for her than sitting there. Molly carried over the large board they used for rolling out dough and dusted it with flour. A few minutes later, Leah was working on the dough, rolling it with smooth, gentle strokes.

She thumped the rolling pin against the board. "I made a mess of it just now, didn't I?"

Molly looked back at the floured board but didn't see anything amiss. "Mess of what?"

"Never mind being polite. I saw your face when I said that about marriage to Aaron."

"Ach, well, I'm sure he'll forget it," she said, trying to comfort her.

"I should have known better." Leah pressed the rolling pin slowly along the dough. "Still, it is time he was thinking about marriage. He needs a wife, and little Becky needs a mother."

"I don't think he'd thank you for saying that." Molly hesitated. All she knew about Aaron's wife was the obvious fact that he'd adored her. "Did you know her well? His first wife, I mean."

Leah paused the movements of the rolling pin. "Not well, no. We weren't seeing much of them at that time. She was very young, very sweet. Pretty, too. And they were both young." She said it was if being young were a disadvantage.

"Too young?" Molly wondered whether Leah had thought she and William were too young.

"No younger than a lot of folks getting married, I guess. But I did wonder how that marriage would work in the long run. Aaron was bright and ambitious—that was one reason for leaving the inn to him. She didn't seem like the person who would take her part in that. But it's hard to say."

"Yah, I guess so." She prodded the chicken with a fork, then turned the burner down. It couldn't be good in a marriage for the partners to be pulling in opposite directions. She nodded toward the screen door. "He's coming."

"I see." Leah handed her the rolling pin. "If you'll give me a fresh towel, I'll cover the dough up to dry. You should be going to the store soon, ain't so?"

Before she could answer, Aaron had heard the comment as he came in.

"Are you going somewhere?" His tone was almost accusing.

She nodded, wondering what fault Aaron could find in her grocery shopping. "I need to go to the grocery store to pick up a few things for the weekend. Is that a problem?"

"I was going—" He stopped, then started again. "It doesn't matter. I was going to take the buggy to pick up Becky, since it's so wet out, but I'll just take her boots along."

"I can do the shopping later—" Molly began, but Leah interrupted her.

"You don't want to do that. It'll make you late getting home. Why don't you both pick up Becky at the schoolhouse and then go to the grocery store? It would be good for Aaron to get reacquainted with Lost Creek. You could show him around."

Aaron's jaw tightened. "I don't think so. Not today."

"It would make a long day for Becky, that's certain sure," Molly said lightly. "Maybe you should look at the shopping list in case there's anything more you want." She put the list in front of Leah, hoping it would turn her thoughts in another direction.

Molly herself was thinking Leah was still being less tactful than usual. It was clear Aaron wanted no more to do with Molly than was needed.

She dusted the flour from her hands and turned down the stove, and Aaron took advantage of the moment to depart in search of Becky's boots.

Molly shook her head, wondering what Leah was thinking. Maybe it was just the result of having been helpless for all this time. A thought struck her, and she drew in a sharp breath as she thought about yesterday's worries. Was her guess correct? Was Leah so eager to throw them together because she was matchmaking? If so, she might just get the opposite effect.

Chapter Six

~~

Molly woke early Friday morning, already thinking of what should be completed before their guests arrived early in the afternoon. She remained still for a moment, wrapped in a cocoon of blankets. There was nothing like sleeping in her own bed to make her feel rested.

That was just as well because there was much to do today. This really was a trial run for Aaron as manager, and she hoped that it went well. She did feel that way, didn't she? Or was there a tiny part of her that wanted to show him up?

Shocked by the idea, she chased it from her mind. This was about Leah, not her. She was grateful for everything Leah had done for her, and now it was time to pass it on. Leah had chosen Aaron, and right now he needed to have something to encourage him.

Still in her bare feet, she crossed the braided rug that had been made by her Great-Aunt Alice and stood at the window. No wonder the daylight was muted—a dense fog covered the valley. That was yet another sign of autumn. Soon the trees would begin to change to their autumn dress, the hills would be alive with color and their reservations book would fill up.

It was an exciting time and one that she loved. But in the

meantime—well, today's events were enough to concentrate on today. Unfortunately, she couldn't quite banish from her mind the thought that had haunted her overnight. Was Leah really trying to matchmake between her and Aaron? The thought clung like a lingering headache. It would make working with him terribly difficult; didn't Leah see that?

Shaking her head, she began to dress, hearing the sounds of Daad and her brothers going out to the barn for the milking, and the clatter of pans in the kitchen beneath her feet. Mamm would be expecting Molly to appear to help with breakfast. If they could have a few moments alone, maybe she could consult Mammi about Leah's actions. That would be the best way of handling it for sure. Mammi would clear her mind, like the fog lifting and dissipating from the valley.

She hurried, but by the time she reached the kitchen, her sisters were there already. There'd be no chance at the moment for a private talk.

Dorie was setting the table, talking the entire time, while Lida carried milk and juice to the table. Dorie, with the best intentions, could never manage to get a full pitcher to the table without dribbling.

Mammi, busy at the stove, was making scrambled eggs and frying scrapple at the same time. Molly took over the scrapple and eggs while her mother checked the coffeepot.

"Dorie, finish up now. They're on their way in."

"Almost done, Mammi." She slapped napkins beside each plate quickly. "Did you hear me say how I helped Becky yesterday? She's like David. Sometimes she needs someone to talk for her."

David, coming in the door, heard that and made a face at his twin. "How do you know she needs you to talk for her? Maybe she just can't get a word in because you babble too much."

Molly and her mother exchanged glances, smiling. Only recently had David shown signs of disputing with Dorie for leadership of the younger ones. Dorie was silent for a moment, shocked, and before she could start again, Daadi was pulling out his chair.

"Sit down, all of you. Some of us have put in a half day's work already, and we're hungry."

"Yah, and some of us put in as much time fixing your breakfast," Mammi said, laughing. She put a mug of coffee in front of him and nodded to Molly to put the platters on the table. Once she was seated, Daadi caught everyone's attention and bowed his head for the silent prayer to start the day.

Mammi had told her once that her morning prayer was always the Lord's Prayer. It covered everything, she said, and finished just when Daadi looked up. Sure enough, as she murmured a silent, "Amen," Daadi settled himself, glanced around, and reached for the scrapple, forking two crispy slices onto his plate.

As usual, he asked what everyone had planned for the day. Mammi had told her once Daad wanted all of them to learn how to set goals for each day. You had, of course, to leave room for the surprises the Lord put in front of you, but he said if you knew where you were headed it was easier to tackle those things.

Conversation bounced around the table as it always did. She wondered for a moment how someone like Aaron would cope with a family like this one. Would he jump into the talk or sit silent, thinking his own thoughts?

She noticed Mammi looking at her several times with

a thoughtful expression on her face. More than once, she thought her mother was going to ask her something, but someone always chimed in first. Usually Dorie, but David was getting in ahead of her often. Mammi had said that sooner or later David would find his voice, and she wondered how much Becky had to do with his speaking up. Molly had seen how often they spoke together. They seemed to be forming a bond.

Breakfast came to an end, and the three youngest ones scrambled to get ready for school. She glanced at the clock. It looked as if she might get her chance to ask Mammi's advice before she had to leave for work. She'd feel much better walking back into the situation with her mother's sound words to fall back on.

No sooner had Mammi waved the young ones off than the others set off for their chores. Molly took up a dish towel as her mother tackled the dishes in the sink. "I have a few minutes to spare. I'll help with these."

Mammi turned on the hot water, and suds came up over the dishes in the sink. "Gut. We can work and talk at the same time." Her mother's smile was knowing. "What is troubling you, daughter?"

"How do you do that?" Molly exclaimed. "You always know what we're thinking about."

"Not what," her mother said. "Just that you are worrying." She clasped Molly's wrist, leaving a few soap bubbles behind. "Tell me."

"You know how excited Leah has been over having Aaron here to take charge of the inn."

"Yah, I know. I wondered how that was working out. Is there a problem?"

Molly considered. How to put it? She didn't want to exaggerate, like Dorie.

When she didn't answer right away, her mother probed a bit. "Isn't he doing as well as she expected?"

"Ach, it's not that, exactly." Now that it came to the point, she was regretting bringing it up.

"What, exactly?" Mamm asked patiently.

"Leah...well, she's not always so good at figuring out people." She gave her mother a teasing smile. "Not like you."

"Poor Leah never had children of her own. The inn, much as she loves it, doesn't teach you about people like children do." Mammi smiled, looking at her fondly. "I can't tell you how much I'd learned from you by the time your brother was born. And then he was so different from you that I had to do it all over again."

"I believe that," she said, laughing a little. Funny. She'd always supposed, in the vague way you wonder sometimes about your elders, that Mammi was proud of her friend Leah's accomplishments. Maybe even a little envious of all she'd done. But she actually sounded sorry for Leah.

"She told me once she was sorry not to have given Isaiah a family," Molly said. "I just wondered if they felt leaving the inn to Aaron was a substitute for that."

"Probably so." Mamm nodded. "But I think she doesn't know him as well as she might, ain't so? What did she do?"

"He was concerned about the things he couldn't teach his daughter. Things she needed a woman for. And Leah told him, jokingly I think, that maybe it was time he looked for another wife. I could see that it upset him."

"Ach, that's a shame. But it's like Leah. She's got it set in her mind that Aaron would be the son they never had. She thinks an innkeeper needs a spouse, so she's trying to make that happen."

Molly nodded. As usual, her mother knew more than it

seemed she could. "I'm afraid she'll push him away if she pushes too much."

"Ach, I should think she'd know better than that. She'll ease off. You'll see."

That wasn't exactly the advice she'd hoped for. "I hoped so when she saw his reaction. She noticed. Nobody could help noticing. Aaron's not ready to think about marrying again. But then she turned around and tried to push us together." She could feel the flush heating her cheeks. "She's matchmaking, Mammi. What am I going to do about it?"

Mammi shook the suds off her hands as she turned toward Molly. "Are you sure? Maybe she was just thinking he needs to make friends here. She probably thinks you'd be good for him."

"Like a medicine?" She really didn't care for that idea.

Her mother laughed at her expression. "No, I mean as a friend. And it's possible she senses he's waking up from that long period of mourning. She does know him better than you do." She squeezed Molly's hand. "Get on with you or you're going to be late. And don't worry. When I see Leah, I'll try to convince her that pushing can bring the opposite of what she wants. After all, if it's the Lord's will, it will work out, no matter what we think of it."

Molly clung to that thought as she started out for the inn. She just hoped her mother was right about it. Now to prepare for their incoming guests. And try really hard to keep everything running smoothly.

By Saturday morning, Aaron was feeling hopeful that he was going to get through the rest of the weekend. Welcoming their guests had gone fine, with Aunt Leah coming out in her wheelchair to greet them and with Molly there to smooth over anything awkward. Probably it was easier because one of the two couples were frequent visitors, knowing what to expect. He'd overheard Mrs. Bradford—Vera, she insisted he call her—telling her friend about Amish customs. She hadn't been right about everything she said, but it wasn't his business to interfere.

He hurried downstairs as soon as he was dressed to find that Becky was already having her breakfast at the kitchen table. He bent to kiss the top of her head. "All by yourself?"

"Molly is taking some things over to the other kitchen. To fix for the visitors." She studied her cereal bowl. "Are they going to be here much longer?"

"Just until tomorrow." He kept his voice casual. Was the idea of other people in the house troubling her? "Have you seen them yet?"

She shook her head fiercely. "Molly says they only talk Englisch." That fact seemed to worry her.

"You speak Englisch very well. You'll be fine."

"No I won't." Her voice rose suddenly. "I won't know what to say to them. I'll forget the Englisch words. I want them to go away."

"Hey, it's all right." Aaron discovered his hand was shaking as he reached out to her. Focusing, he put his hand on her shoulder, feeling the edge of her shoulder blade and the small bones of her arm. They seemed as fragile as a bird's wing. "You don't have to see them. You can stay up in your room if you want."

That seemed to comfort her. She picked up her dish and took it to the sink. "I will."

Molly, coming in with a tray in her hands, must have heard this. She nodded to Aaron and started putting bread and muffins on the tray. "I thought you might come to the other kitchen and help me. Would that be okay?"

He wasn't sure whether that question was aimed at him or Becky. He started to say that he'd already made plans for his daughter, but Becky spoke first. "What could I do?"

"You could put some muffins on the table in a basket," Molly said. "And wash some of the fruit I'm cutting up."

"I don't think…" he began, but Becky had already nodded.

"Okay. I can do that."

He just looked at her. What had happened to the little girl who'd been almost crying a moment ago?

Molly smiled at him as if she knew what he was thinking. "Right." She pushed the swinging door with her elbow, and they both went through.

Left alone in the kitchen, Aaron reached for the coffee-pot, put it down without using it, and headed after them. He guessed they were all helping. Molly seemed to have all the answers, and he didn't know if he was annoyed or pleased.

Becky waited for him at the door. "I'm going to wash the fruit, Daadi. Molly says you can put the napkins on the table by the plates and get out the juice pitchers."

It sounded as if Molly didn't have much confidence in his ability to help. That was probably justified. He glanced around at Molly as he dispensed napkins. "Isn't Hilda here to help?"

"She'll be down as soon as she tidies the guest rooms."

Maybe they needed to rearrange the schedule. But there was no time to think about it because the guests were coming in, talking cheerfully with each other. Becky, startled at the sound of their voices, whispered something to Molly, who nodded. With an apprehensive look at their guests,

Becky slipped out the door to the safety of the private part of the house.

Vera Bradford, trim and elegant with her silver-gray curls and bright lipstick, looked younger than her square red-faced husband. She was discussing plans for the day with the other couple. Her husband's main interest was apparently his breakfast, and he waited impatiently and then looked at the menu Aaron handed him in surprise.

"What's this?" he demanded.

"We thought you might like to order what you want. Molly will be happy to cook whatever you want."

Vera studied the menu, frowning. "Molly, where is that delicious cereal mix that you always have with yogurt? I always look forward to it."

If Molly was thrown off balance, she didn't show it. "Yah, of course, we have it. I'll get it out in just a moment. What would you like for your main course?"

"What about those Amish breakfast casseroles you always make?" her husband demanded. "Like the one that has all the sausages in it."

"George, you know the doctor says you shouldn't have sausage, anyway." Vera sounded as if she were used to placating her husband.

"Maybe you'd like some fried scrapple," Molly said. "That's a genuine Amish breakfast—my father and brothers had it just this morning when they came in from milking. I think you'd like it."

"Well... I guess. And some scrambled eggs and toast and..."

"And fruit," his wife said firmly.

George gave in, nodding, and the dissatisfaction around the table slipped away, but Aaron heard the man muttering something about going to a motel if he wanted to sit there and order scrambled eggs.

Aaron could only hope his face didn't show the embarrassment he was feeling. He had to tell Molly how sorry he was. She'd tried to talk him out of it, but he hadn't listened. Maybe she should have tried harder, but he hadn't given her a chance, had he?

He quickly discovered another reason why the menus were a mistake—Molly was kept running from one thing to another, trying to cook four different meals at once. He tried to help her, but his lack of kitchen skills made him more of a hindrance.

"Why don't you get the large container of grain cereal mix from the pantry?" she suggested after he'd dropped two eggs on the floor trying to get them into the pan. "The yogurt is in the refrigerator."

Relieved, he headed for the pantry. Maybe there he'd find a bucket of water to stick his head in. That was where he belonged.

Molly checked on the pan of cookies in the oven, letting out an aroma that at home would bring the kinder running from every part of the house. There was only one child at the inn, and Becky was already beside her. Standing on a wooden chair, she rolled a ball of dough and then carefully set it on a cookie sheet.

"They smell so gut," she said, looking up at Molly. "They're for the visitors, ain't so?"

Her wistful look wasn't lost on Molly. "We'll share with them, yah. But I think we'll have to have some first." She put on a mock serious expression. "We want to make sure they're good enough for our guests. That's called taste testing."

Becky giggled. "I'll be gut at that."

"You surely will." That little giggle of Becky's didn't come too often, but when it did, Molly's heart seemed to swell. Becky had truly warmed up in the last few days, and Molly could only pray that nothing would happen to cause a setback.

As if she were thinking about the same thing, Becky said, "I like it here." She hesitated. "But I think the visitors are a little bit scary."

Molly warned herself to approach the subject with care. "Why is that? They seem okay to me."

Becky stared silently at the cookies Molly was sliding from the hot pan to the cooling rack and didn't think the child was going to answer at first. But then her soft voice sounded.

"They talk so loud. And what if they ask me something?" Her voice trembled as she asked the question.

Such a simple thing, one would think, but it wasn't simple to Becky. She had probably not been around Englisch people much before. Fortunately, Molly knew exactly how she felt, because she'd been just like that once upon a time.

"When I was about your age, we had a barn raising at our house. Lots of neighbors came, and some of them were Englischers. Mammi was wonderful busy, and she said I could help her on the day. I could take snacks around to the workers, and my brother could take the water bucket and dipper. He was worried that he might spill the water, but I was worried that they'd ask me something. What would I say? What if I didn't understand them?"

Becky's eyes were wide. "What did you do?"

"Mammi helped me. She said mostly people would ask my name or how old I was, so we should practice that. So she pretended to be an Englisch person and asked the questions. She made her voice sound different ways—sometimes low and gruff and sometimes high and silly. It made us both laugh, but I practiced. I said my name and I said how old I was, and I practiced in Deutsch and in Englisch. And then I wasn't afraid anymore."

From the corner of her eye, Molly saw the door into the kitchen move just a little. Aaron stood silently, watching and listening. He'd think she was silly, or even interfering, but she couldn't stop now.

So she asked Becky in the lowest voice she could, "What is your name, little girl?"

Another voice spoke behind them, in a much lower voice, as Aaron repeated the question. Becky spun around on her chair, her face lit with laughter. "Daadi, you sound silly."

"Maybe so, but what's the answer?" He came close to them, putting his hand gently on Becky's shoulder.

Becky stood up straight and spoke in careful Englisch. "My name is Becky. I am eight years old."

Molly clapped, laughing, and wonderfully relieved that Aaron had joined in. Did he realize how much Becky's mood was affected by his? It was as if the child had an extra layer of sensitivity to the only parent she had.

Aaron picked up his daughter and spun her around in the most spontaneous gesture she'd seen from him yet. Then, still holding her in his arms, he turned to Molly.

"If you can't think of anything else to say, you can always say, 'I'll ask Molly.' Ain't so?"

Becky nodded vigorously.

Aaron set her down. "Will you go see if Aunt Leah wants anything?"

"Yah, for sure." Becky almost danced as she darted off

to find Leah. Aaron turned to Molly, and the expression in his eyes made her heart give an echoing thump.

She rushed to speak before he could say whatever he was thinking. "Since tomorrow is the off Sunday for worship, we can do breakfast as usual. And my Mamm and Daad want everyone to come over for a picnic after the guests check out."

That seemed to give him something else to think about, and she felt relieved. It was best that he didn't say something he'd regret later.

"That's gut of them. We'll have to see if Aunt Leah feels up to it. We can easily take the wheelchair in the buggy."

She slid cooled cookies onto a platter for the guests. "That's what my mother thought. Or she would send someone over with the wagon if it doesn't fit in the buggy."

Molly really wanted this to work out. The picnic would give her mother and Leah a chance to talk. Then Mamm could discourage Leah's matchmaking efforts before they exploded in her face.

Picking up the platter, Molly turned to carry it into the dining room for their usual afternoon guest snack, but before she could move, Aaron's hand closed around her wrist. Her startled gaze met his. The platter tilted, and he steadied it with his other hand.

"Denke, Molly." His voice was soft, and it sent a tremor down her spine. "I made a big mistake in not listening to you. Breakfast could have been a disaster as a result of my ideas. And instead of blaming me, you saved the day."

She shook her head quickly. "It was nothing."

His fingers moved on her wrist. "Yah, it was something. Something very good. I'll try to remember it. It's like I said to Becky. Always listen to Molly."

Her gaze met his again, and for a moment she couldn't possibly say anything. The air between them seemed to tremble. Then she heard Becky running back to them, and she pulled away. She couldn't be feeling what she thought she was. She couldn't.

Chapter Seven

Their guests had finally left on Sunday with many compliments and promises to come back. The changes that had caused problems seemed to be forgotten, and Molly could only be grateful. It could have been worse, yah?

Aaron seemed to have forgotten those strained moments between them over the failure of his ideas. Just as well to forget and move on, she supposed. Or maybe Aaron hadn't felt anything. Maybe the flare of attraction and the way the silence between them shimmered had been all in her mind. If so, it was time she took control of her imagination. She wasn't looking for romance again. She'd already had that, and look how it had turned out.

Aaron lifted Leah to the rear seat of the buggy, and Molly couldn't help but see the fear in Leah's eyes when Aaron picked her up. Poor Leah. She wasn't used to depending on others for things she once did easily herself, and it must be alarming to trust.

"You're fine," Molly said hurriedly, hoping Aaron hadn't seen her expression. "Just lean back against this pillow that Becky brought for you."

Once she was sure she'd been settled, Leah managed to relax. "Yah, gut. Denke, Aaron. And thanks to you, too, Becky."

Leah reached forward to pat Becky's shoulder where she sat in the front seat, and Becky smiled, hardly able to contain her excitement. Molly suspected her cheerfulness had to do with going to see Dorie and David, but whatever the cause, she was happy.

Meanwhile, Aaron had folded the wheelchair. He slid it behind them, wedging it to be sure it wouldn't bump against the back of Leah's seat. Molly climbed nimbly up to sit next to Leah, reaching back to grab the wheelchair and secure it in place.

"All set," she said quickly, and Aaron nodded, then took his place in the driver's seat. A click to the horse, and they were on their way.

"We have everything?" He glanced toward the back seat.

"We're fine." Leah sounded a little testy, no doubt feeling nervous about her first excursion since she'd come home from the hospital.

"And I packed up the leftover cookies," Molly added. "In case anyone was wondering."

Becky giggled. "David and Dorie will want some."

"I'm sure." Molly thought again how glad she was for the friendship between Becky and the twins. It had been good for all three of them, but especially for Becky.

As for her other concern... Molly told herself firmly that Aaron either hadn't noticed those moments between them or had decided to ignore them. That was fine by her. She certainly didn't want their business relationship complicated by emotional reactions on anyone's part.

Besides, whatever she'd imagined between herself and Aaron, it wasn't remotely like the thrill of what she'd once felt for Will. So they were fine. Just...friends, she guessed.

Leah gasped as a car spun by them on the narrow road,

but Aaron's hands remained steady on the lines. "It's all right," he said, obviously having heard her.

"Of course, it is," Leah snapped.

Molly managed not to roll her eyes. Leah would settle down once they'd reached the picnic, she felt sure. And beyond that, she was relying on her mother to change Leah's attitude toward matchmaking.

They were soon pulling up to the back porch. Molly wasn't surprised to find the whole family outside to greet them. Her mother would have reminded them this was Leah's first outing. If there was something to celebrate, Mammi made it special, even if it was a star on a spelling test.

Her brother Joshua took the porch steps in a single stride and tied the buggy horse to the hitching rail. "Wilkom. I'm Josh, Molly's bruder." He reached up to shake hands with Aaron and then turned his attention to Leah. "Leah, may I lift you down? I promise not to drop you."

Josh had always been a favorite of Leah's, and her frown dissolved in a smile. "That's what you said when you wanted to carry that pan of brownies."

Josh grinned. "Have a heart. I was only eight at the time."

Meanwhile, Dorie and David clasped hands with Becky. "Mammi, can we show Becky the new kittens?" Dorie claimed the barn cat didn't mind her touching her kittens, but the scratches on her hand proved otherwise.

"No touching," Mamm said firmly. She smiled at Becky. "They're pretty little things, but the mamma doesn't want them touched yet. So just look."

Becky nodded seriously, and the smile in her eyes suggested she hadn't seen very small kittens before. The three of them darted off to the barn.

Aaron started to call something to his daughter, then glanced at Molly, as if asking if it was all right. She nodded. Dorie sometimes skirted around things she shouldn't do, but she wouldn't disobey Mamm's direct orders.

Leah allowed Josh and Aaron to carry her between them up the porch steps, while Daad and Lida set up the wheelchair on the porch. "One day we'll have to put up a ramp," Daad said, eyeing the porch as if measuring for one. "It's a wonder none of you kinder has broken a bone yet."

"Don't be silly, Daadi. You know we're careful," Lida said pertly. Daadi laughed and hugged her.

"Careful, indeed. You're anything but that." He swung her around and dropped her by the door. "You hold the door while we help Leah inside."

In a few minutes, everyone but the young ones had gathered around the rectangular wooden table, its top faded and scarred from hundreds of family meals. Conversation flew around the kitchen as Lida started pouring iced tea while Mammi talked about baked bean recipes with Leah and Daad, Josh and Aaron retired to the window corner, talking about the fall harvest as Daad gestured toward the pasture.

Noticing that the picnic table under the apple tree wasn't set, Molly raised her eyebrows at her mother. "Not eating outside?"

"I thought inside might be more comfortable for Leah, ain't so?" She looked at Leah as she spoke, and for a moment Leah looked ready to object. Then her expression dissolved into a smile.

"Yah, I guess so. When I get out of this chair, it'll be easier." She smacked her hands on the chair arms.

Already Leah was mellowing, it seemed. Molly relaxed a little, glancing from Leah to her mother. The look was meant to remind her to speak to Leah about the matchmaking, but as far as Molly could see, her mother didn't respond.

Maybe she was exaggerating the situation. Perhaps what she'd taken for hints on Leah's part were just her natural longing to run everything. But it still bothered her.

Lida carried a glass of iced tea to Leah and then to Aaron. As she started toward Molly, they heard a shout from the barn. Molly looked through the screen door, and her heart seemed to jump into her throat. It was David, running and shouting at the same time.

"Komm, schnell! It's Becky."

Aaron shoved past her, sending an angry glare her way. And then she was running, too, and praying. Becky. *Please Lord, keep Becky safe.*

He never should have let Becky go off alone with those kinder. What was he thinking? It was one thing to play with them at school, where someone's eyes were on them, but not alone. They'd got up to something.

He spared some anger for Molly, who had tacitly approved. But the fault was his, all his. If she was hurt—he'd promised Rachel he'd keep her safe.

Bursting into the barn, Molly was right behind him as he tried to see everything at once. His gaze flew to Becky. She was standing on the railing that formed the top of the haymow, and she was frozen, obviously afraid to move, afraid to fall.

Dorie, also on the railing, held out her hands to Becky, probably encouraging her to take a step. He rushed across the wide planks that formed the barn floor—as hard as cement after all these years. He was afraid to speak, afraid his voice would break…

"Goodness, what are you up to?" Molly sounded as if nothing at all was wrong. "It's all right, Becky. You're safe."

Safe? If he'd ever felt like hitting someone, he felt it now. He wouldn't, but he felt it. Brushing Molly aside, he reached his daughter and gathered her up in his arms, holding her close.

"It's all right, sweet girl. I have you."

Molly reached toward Becky, but whatever she intended to say, he didn't want to hear it. Aaron swung away, turning his back on her.

The others rushed into the barn, and he could hear Aunt Leah shouting, asking what was wrong. Molly's mother turned back for a moment, calling out that Becky was fine.

Fine! She's been scared to death. Aaron held her close, thinking the same words over and over. He'd promised Rachel he'd keep her safe. He'd promised.

Dorie scrambled down the four-or five-foot-high rail. She stared at the floor, avoiding everyone's eyes.

"Whose idea was this?" Caleb Esch, Molly's father, had a deep voice that was surprising coming from his lean frame.

Dorie's lips were clamped, and she didn't look up. David frowned at his twin, and then joined her in staring at the floor.

"Well, Dorie?" He didn't hesitate to name the culprit. He knew his *kinder* too well for that.

Dorie's lips trembled. "I'm sorry." The words burst out. "I didn't know Becky would be scared. We walk along the railing all the time."

Becky's tears were dripping on his shirt. What he wanted to do was take his daughter home and stay there. But he couldn't. The relationship between Aunt Leah and the Esch family was too deep for that to be an answer.

Dorie sniffled a little. She walked toward him, her feet dragging. She stopped and seemed to force herself to look up. "I'm sorry, Becky. I thought you'd like to climb on it."

David took a step toward her, glaring at his twin.

Dorie seemed to get the message and sniffled again. "I'm sorry I said you were a scaredy cat. I didn't mean it."

Becky wiped her wet cheeks on his shirt. "It's okay," she murmured.

His daughter had forgiven. It was embarrassing that he couldn't manage to do the same. Becky wiggled, and Aaron let her go reluctantly. She stood next to him, not quite ready to let go of his hand yet.

Caleb looked at his daughter and sighed. "Dorie, go up to your room until I call you. We'll talk about it later."

Dorie nodded and scurried off toward the house, and Molly's mother gestured toward the barn door. "We'd best go relieve Leah's worries," she said, the good humor returning to her face. "And supper is about ready."

Aaron thought again that he'd like to snatch up Becky and go home. Then he realized she was no longer hanging onto him. She'd gone over to Caleb and tugged at his pant leg.

Caleb's face creased in a smile, and he bent down so that his face was even with hers. "What is it, Becky?"

"Dorie," she whispered, and didn't seem able to go any further.

Caleb studied her face and seemed to understand. "You don't want her to miss the picnic, ain't so?"

She nodded vigorously.

He patted her shoulder. "It's all right. I promise. I'll call her down when we're ready to eat. Would you like to sit beside her?"

Becky nodded again, with a glance at David.

"Yah, between Dorie and David. Just so."

Caleb must have just the right touch because Becky, his shy little Becky, took his hand, and they walked off to the house together.

Aaron watched them, bemused. The Esch family seemed to have an odd effect on both of them.

Molly didn't have an opportunity to speak to Aaron privately until the next day, and maybe that was just as well. Judging by the severe expression he'd worn when he sat down at the supper table, he hadn't been thinking favorably about anybody in the Esch family.

If only Dorie hadn't jumped into trouble with both feet.... but it was useless to think that. Dorie was just being herself. She was a natural leader, and usually other kinder followed her. And most of them would have wobbled along the railing or jumped off. But Becky was different.

How different? Why? Molly considered that the next morning as she walked over to the office. Leah had slept in after yesterday's exertions, and Aaron was walking Becky to school. She'd have time to bring the reservation book up-to-date and check the rooms for anything the guests might have left behind before either of them needed her.

But instead of thinking about work, she found she was considering the situation with Becky and the other kinder in a new light. It wasn't her imagination—Becky was not only shy, but she wasn't used to playing with other kids her age. Or, it seemed, in trying new things.

Everyone seemed to think that was related to losing her mother, but somehow Molly was beginning to think it wasn't that simple.

Not your business, she told herself, opening the reservation book on the desk in the office. Aaron would not welcome interference with his daughter. She ought to back away, but how could she?

Will used to say her heart was like butter, melting for anyone in trouble. Her jaw tightened at the thought. Maybe so, but she'd rather have a heart of butter than a heart of stone. She couldn't see Becky and her father every day without wanting to help them.

The door opened behind her and Aaron came in, carrying a mug of coffee in each hand. He set one down in front of her. "One sugar and no milk, yah?"

It might be a peace offering, so she accepted it with a smile. "Just right. Denke. You're back early, aren't you?"

He nodded, and she thought he looked puzzled. "Your sister Lida was waiting for us at the lane. She said she'd take Becky. She offered to come for her every day."

"That's nice of her." Lida was unpredictable at times, bouncing from being thoughtless to jumping in to help.

"Did you put her up to that?" Aaron's voice was sharp, as if she'd done something wrong.

"No." She suspected her tone said she was annoyed. "But if I had, would there be something wrong with that?"

He shrugged his shoulders as if that was an answer.

"I don't know what that means." She felt like telling him to use his words, like Mammi did when the kinder tried to avoid talking. "If I had, it would be because I care about Becky. But I didn't, so I guess that means Lida does, too."

His lips twitched, and he put up his hands as if to shield himself. "All right. I didn't mean anything. It's just that I don't know Lida."

Her aggravation with him shriveled like a popped balloon. "Nobody knows Lida these days. She's twelve going on twenty, I think…a little girl one day and a young lady the next. Whenever I get exasperated with Lida, my mother tells me I was worse."

"What do you say to that?"

"I tell her just wait until Dorie hits that age. Can you imagine?"

Aaron's smile relaxed his face, and he leaned against the desk, cradling his coffee mug between his hands. "I'd like to have seen you then."

"No, you wouldn't." She laughed, shaking her head. "It's an impossible age for girls. But if Lida says she'll do something, she'll do it, if that's what you're wondering about."

"Becky seemed to like the idea. She skipped off with Lida without a backward glance."

She thought she heard a little regret in his voice. "That's natural enough for an eight-year-old, ain't so?"

"I guess that's true. I just…" He seemed to realize he was on the verge of confiding in her and pulled back. "I wanted to offer to pay Lida, but I didn't know—"

Molly shook her head decisively. "My parents wouldn't want that. She's doing what she should for a neighbor." She could see that he wasn't convinced, and she leaned toward him, trying to make him see. "That's what they're trying to teach her…well, all of us. Money would get in the way."

He looked down at her face and seemed to forget what he was going to say for a moment. "But I should repay her in some way."

"Not with money," she said firmly. "Tell you what, though. Her birthday is next month. Becky could give her a little present. Just something small, mind."

Faced with her firmness, Aaron gave in. "All right. If

you say so." He grinned. "But you'll have to tell us what it should be. Neither of us would know what to get for a brand-new teenager."

"I'll do that." She smiled, glad she'd found a solution he could accept. Still, his attitude toward something so simple made her wonder about his past, as well as Becky's. What made them the way they were?

"I don't know much about kids," Aaron said. "I was usually glad to be the only one, but now...well, I think I envy you for your siblings."

"Most of the time I enjoy them, but sometimes they make my head spin. Like yesterday." She hesitated, wondering if it was safe to bring that up. She sucked in a breath and went on. "Would I be right in thinking Becky hasn't spent much time with other kids?"

His face clouded. "What makes you think that?"

No, it looked as if it hadn't been safe, and Molly wondered how she was going to get out of the situation without starting another quarrel.

"I just thought maybe that accounted for her shyness, that's all." She studied his face, hoping for a breakthrough.

"She saw other children in school every day." He sounded...what? *Defensive*, she thought. "We didn't have any neighbors with kinder, and my parents kept to themselves."

If she had any sense, she'd let the subject drop. "What about your wife's family?"

He didn't answer, and she bit her lip. One of Mammi's favorite sayings was that the tongue was very small, but it could cause very big problems. Too bad she hadn't paid attention.

"Rachel was the youngest in her family." He said the words as if each one cost him money. "Her brothers and sisters were much older. So their kinder were too old to be friends with Becky."

Molly nodded, not speaking. She'd gotten into trouble through talking so she'd best be still.

"Becky always had me," he said firmly. "I made sure of that."

She thought that was all, but it turned out he had something else to say.

"Rachel told me…" He stared out the window, but she couldn't tell what he was seeing. "When she was dying, she told me to take care of Becky. So that's what I do."

Clutching his cup, he walked quickly out of the office. She heard his footsteps receding down the hall, leaving her alone.

Molly took a deep breath and exhaled it slowly, trying to relax her muscles. She felt like banging her head against the desk, but that wouldn't do either her or the desk any good.

Well, she'd asked for it, and she got it. Aaron was taking care of his daughter and doing it so thoroughly he protected her from everything that made life normal for an eight-year-old. He thought he was keeping his promise to his wife. And there was no room in his life for any other relationship.

Leah and her matchmaking were doomed to fail. She just hoped Leah could accept it.

Chapter Eight

Leah, having gotten up late, was making up for it when Molly returned to the kitchen. She'd pulled her wheelchair up to the table and was shuffling several lists in front of her.

"Molly, there you are. Hilda said you were working in the office."

Hilda, safely out of Leah's sight at the pantry door, rolled her eyes at Molly—probably a message, but Molly wasn't sure what it meant. Maybe that Leah's mood needed watching.

"Yah, just checking on a few reservations that came in today. People trying to guess when the leaves are going to be at their peak."

"Third week in October, that's my prediction," Leah said. "Anyone have another guess?" She glanced from Molly to Hilda as if daring them to disagree.

"That's what the almanac says for this year, too," Hilda said.

Molly nodded in agreement. "Probably, but I never make predictions, even when prospective guests ask me to. We're innkeepers, not weather prophets, ain't so?"

All three of them laughed, and the atmosphere in the kitchen seemed to lighten.

"What's funny?" Aaron said, coming in from the porch.

"Molly." Leah clasped his hand. "Forget about that. I want to talk to you about something."

Taking advantage of the moment, Hilda slipped around Leah and walked past Molly, pausing for a whisper. "She's raring to go, and we're supposed to be her hands and feet so watch out."

Molly nodded, trying to keep her face straight. It stood to reason this might happen. Leah's excursion yesterday had given her confidence, Molly supposed, that she was on the mend. And ready to run everything and everyone. She hoped Aaron was prepared for it.

Leah patted the lists she'd been working on. "Here are some things we need from town. Molly, I want you to take Aaron with you." Before Molly could object, Leah swept on. "I know it doesn't take two, but it's important that Aaron meets these people." She waved her lists. "I want you to introduce him around, Molly. See that folks have a chance to see that you're working together now. Right?"

Molly nodded, knowing it was no use arguing with Leah when she was in this mood. But Aaron obviously didn't understand.

"I can do that any time. It's doesn't take two of us to do this shopping." He held up the papers that Leah handed to him. "I want to get to work on the shed roof before that leak gets any worse."

"There's plenty of time for that." Leah waved his objections aside, and Molly decided to get herself out of the way. It seemed likely that Leah and her nephew were going to clash now and then, but she didn't want to see it.

Murmuring something about hitching up the buggy, she slipped out and crossed the lawn to the barn, hearing their voices fade behind her.

Gus, the elderly buggy horse, didn't look enthusiastic when he saw her pull the buggy out and lay out the harness. "Now don't you argue," she told him, and he pricked his ears as if he were listening. "No use arguing when Leah's in that mood. I know from experience."

"You might be right." For just an instant, she felt as shocked as if Gus had spoken.

She turned around and shook her head at Aaron. "You must have given up quickly," she said, smiling.

"No use arguing with a willful woman," he said. He reached for the stall door a moment after she did, and she tightened her grip on the handle.

"I've got it," she said quickly. He seemed to have forgotten those emotional moments when he'd told her about his wife, but she hadn't. And she'd rather not have any more time alone with him just now.

He tried to brush her hand away, and she resisted. "I'll bring Gus out."

"Another willful woman," he said, his lips twitching.

Molly could feel the flush coming up in her cheeks and tried to treat it lightly. "Gus and I were having a nice conversation when you came in."

"I heard. All about the uselessness of arguing."

"That's right." She positioned Gus in front of the stall, and they moved simultaneously to pick up the opposite sides of the harness. She shook her head. "Yesterday seems to have been good for Leah. She's all fired up to get going today."

"I noticed." His tone was noncommittal. "It's good if that means she's feeling better, but I hope she doesn't overdo it."

"Yah, I know." She looked at him seriously, hoping he meant that the way it sounded. "Leah is likely to overdo it, but the physical therapist can usually head her off. It's harder for the rest of us." Would he sense the warning in her words?

"You know her better than I do, for all that she's my aunt." He reached for the buckle strap. "What does it take to get her to listen?"

"Tact," she said. "Lots of tact. Sometimes my mamm can get her to be sensible. Mamm's an old friend besides being sensible herself."

He patted Gus, then swung himself up to the seat. "I guess we're ready." Aaron reached down to help her up, clicked to the horse, and they started down the lane. He didn't speak again until they turned onto the main road.

When Aaron did speak, he went back to her previous comment. "I'm sensible enough, but I don't think being tactful is all that easy for me."

There didn't seem to be any good answer to that. She could hardly say that she agreed with him.

Aaron glanced at her face. "Your silence speaks volumes. You might as well agree with me."

Molly smiled, shaking her head a little. "The thing is that Leah thinks she knows best for everyone. It can be hard to convince her otherwise. But as far as the inn goes, I think she'll let you try anything you want."

"Like changing the breakfast menus? We saw how that worked out."

"You can't expect to know about our guests at the first try. It takes a little time."

"Denke, Molly. But sometimes I wonder if Aunt Leah will ever be able to let go of the reins." He gestured with the lines, and Gus gave him a reproachful look. "All right, Gus. I know you don't like that." He shifted his gaze to Molly. "You're right, it is tempting to talk to him."

She nodded. "Just try to be patient with Leah. Tell Gus anything you like. Or you can tell me. But save your patience for your aunt."

That was the best she could do. She didn't know when or if Leah would stop trying to run things. Or if Aaron's patience would survive having Leah try to set him up with a wife.

Aaron slowed up as they reached the edge of town. Lost Creek wasn't very big, but the mix of buggies and cars always meant cautious driving—to him, at least, if not necessarily to every driver...especially the young ones. Amish or Englisch, they were both likely to take risks.

Molly unfolded the list and glanced through it. "Goodness! Your aunt must want you to meet every Amish merchant in town."

"I noticed." They passed the post office and a row of shops. "I guess next she'll want me to visit every farm. You might think I was running for office."

Molly chuckled. "I'm sure she wants you to feel at home. But they'll all be at worship on Sunday, so anyone you miss today, you can meet then. Look to the right." She leaned forward, pointing. "The ground slopes down there, and you can see the river."

He nodded. He'd remembered that the town was built along the river from his earlier visits. When this part of Pennsylvania was settled, boats were probably the easiest way to get from place to place.

"The water level is about back to normal," Molly said, following it with her gaze. "It got pretty low in August when we didn't have any rain for a couple of weeks."

"Aunt Leah mentioned it. She wants everything to look

perfect for the autumn visitors. But even Aunt Leah can't bend the weather to her will."

Molly shot him a quick glance, maybe wondering if he was being sarcastic. He didn't mean to be, but he'd already seen Aunt Leah's desire to have everything work out the way she wanted it.

"If you'll just go on down Main Street, the store that belongs to Daniel and Beth Miller will be on your right, just outside town."

"What kind of store? I hope we're going to buy something, and not just go in to introduce me." This situation seemed to feel normal to Molly, but he really preferred meeting people one at a time.

"Don't worry about that." The smile in Molly's voice told him she knew just what was troubling him. "There are always things you'll want there. They carry mostly dented cans of food at cheaper prices, along with all sorts of groceries and hardware. You never know what you're going to find there."

"You sound excited about it. Looking for something special?"

"No, I just like to be surprised by what they have. Once we saw a can of pickled sweet potatoes. Josh said he'd eat them if I bought them." Her green eyes danced with laughter. "He ended up feeding them to the pig. Besides, I'm looking forward to talking to Beth."

"So you can tell her all about me, I suppose." There was an edge to his voice that he hadn't intended, but Molly just smiled, much as if he were one of her young siblings talking sassy.

"I might just do that. There's the store just ahead. You can pull in on the side to the hitching rail."

With a cautious look behind him, Aaron made the turn. Gus moved up to the hitching rail and stopped without the need of any guidance from him. Obviously, he'd been here before.

Clutching the list, Molly hopped down from the buggy seat before he could help her. She rubbed Gus's face, telling him he was a good boy, and then started inside. Aaron walked behind her, feeling as if he were going on display.

A man he assumed was Daniel Miller walked to the counter at the sound of the shop bell, and then broke into a smile when he saw who it was. "Beth, look who's here," he called toward the back of the store.

His wife came hurrying toward them, smiling and holding out her hands to Molly. "Ach, Molly this is a nice surprise." They hugged. Molly seemed to get that kind of welcome with everyone she met.

"Molly doesn't need to introduce you." The tall rugged-looking man held out a hand to Aaron. "You must be Leah's nephew, Aaron, yah? I'm Dan Miller."

"Gut to meet you, Dan. How did you know? Did my Aunt Leah call ahead?"

Dan chuckled. "No, but the Amish grapevine in Lost Creek is alive and well. I don't know how they do it, but those women get the word around."

Smiling, his wife swatted his arm playfully. "You know better than that. Just go into the hardware store and listen to the men gossiping."

Dan turned to him as if sharing a secret. "You know she's right, but I'll never admit it."

A moment later, Dan had snatched the list from Molly and handed it to a teenage girl who was waiting nearby.

"Anna, you'll take care of this, ain't so? Just say so if you don't understand something."

The girl nodded, smiling. After taking a good long look at Aaron, she hurried off to the shelves.

Dan must have noticed his reaction. "They'll stop staring at you eventually," he said.

"It can't be soon enough for me." He realized he was relaxing in the friendly atmosphere of the shop and the people.

Molly and Beth had their heads together. "I'm going back to see the baby," Molly said, and the two of them headed down the aisle.

"Young Daniel is in his basket at the back corner of the room," Dan explained. "How he can sleep with the bell going and folks talking I don't know, but he manages." The pride in his voice made it clear that the baby could do no wrong in his father's eyes.

Aaron leaned over the basket, knowing he'd best say something complimentary about the tiny boy wrapped in a blue shawl. His cheeks were round and rosy, and he slept with a kind of serious intensity that reminded him of Becky at that age. After he made a few suitable remarks, he and Dan became engrossed in finding the type of latch Aaron needed for a stall door.

He and Dan went back to the counter just as the teenager appeared with two full shopping bags. It looked like they were finished, but apparently Molly wasn't ready to leave the baby yet. He was wondering if he should go looking for her when she appeared in the center aisle of the shop. She held the baby in her arms, and her face—which Aaron had considered pretty from the moment he saw her—right now glowed with beauty as she looked at the boppli.

Something stirred in his heart, and he thought again that Will must have been ferhoodled to walk away from a woman like Molly.

Once they were back in the buggy with their purchases stacked behind them, Aaron felt more than ready to go home. He glanced at Molly. "Can't we skip the rest of it?"

She raised her eyebrows. "Only if you want to explain why to your aunt Leah."

"You have a point. Okay, what's next?"

"We're meant to stop at the coffee shop. Lydia Fisher runs it, and her husband helps out when he can. He has a carpentry business, so he's pretty busy."

"Are we buying something or just looking for introductions?" He could see that Molly was enjoying their trotting around town. Well, that made at least one of them.

Molly's soft chuckle made him smile in spite of himself. "We're supposed to have coffee and a cruller. And the crullers are your aunt's favorites, so we'd best bring a half-dozen back with us."

He'd argue the subject, but Molly had been right. He wouldn't want to explain why they hadn't finished the list.

"Was this what you meant by being patient with my aunt?" he asked, and watched her face as she pondered the question.

"I was thinking more about the business, but I guess it does include this."

He nodded. Patience wasn't a strength of his, but he had to admit that spending time with Molly wasn't exactly a hardship.

A few minutes later, they were at a small corner table in the coffee shop, being waited on by Lydia Fisher, a round pretty woman with rosy cheeks and a friendly smile.

The coffee was hot and strong, and the crullers were crisp and delicious. "Not so bad, is it?" Molly teased.

Before he had a chance to reply, he was interrupted by the arrival at their table of a stout middle-aged woman who watched them as if fascinated by the sight of them.

"Now, don't let me interrupt you two." She gave an arched look at Molly. "Dear Molly is so sweet, and you're Leah's own nephew. It just couldn't be more suitable. We're all so very happy."

She continued burbling along, but Aaron had stopped listening as something became clear in his mind. Here was an explanation for all the things that niggled at him. He should have seen it before—Aunt Leah telling him how much he needed a wife, pushing him together with Molly at every opportunity. And Molly herself going along with it and telling him to be patient.

His aunt had decided he needed a wife to run her precious inn, and she'd handpicked the one she thought was the best candidate. She was matchmaking, and Molly was going along with it. Well, they'd soon learn when they'd gone too far. He'd be having a showdown with both of them as soon as they returned to the inn.

As soon as they were on their way back, Molly tried to speak. But what could she say? A few careless words from the biggest blabbermaul in the district, and all Leah's precious plans were blown to bits. Ruth Byler delighted in gossip, and everyone knew that. Why had Leah decided to confide in her, when she hadn't talked to either Molly or her mamm?

Molly guessed she knew the answer to that question. Ruth was one of their volunteers, helping out when needed to stay with Leah at night. If Leah had been wakeful and the two of them had been talking in the wee hours of the morning, how tempting it might have been to Leah to share her dreams for the future.

Molly tried to swallow the lump in her throat. If Leah had said anything about it to her, she would certainly have put Leah right about Molly marrying anybody in the near future. Maybe someday, she thought, if God sent the right person into her life. But not now.

As for Aaron, surely he had made it plain that his heart still belonged to the wife he'd lost. Even Leah should have seen that, shouldn't she?

Her mother would certain sure have pointed out to Leah that her involvement could backfire and create problems for all of them. And that was exactly what had happened.

She risked a sideways glance at him. Aaron stared straight ahead, his face frozen so hard that it might have been carved out of wood. She'd never seen a chin so tight or lips so clenched.

Flexing her own lips, she wondered if her mouth would even form the words. "Aaron…"

It came out in the merest whisper, drowned by the sound of the wheels on the blacktop road. She cleared her throat. She had to do better than that.

"Aaron…"

His glare was enough to silence the howl of a wolf. "I don't want to hear it."

"But you have to. You don't understand."

His hands tightened on the reins, and Gus tossed his head, objecting.

"I understand very well. I wish I didn't. I'm not going

over this twice. I'll do whatever talking I have to do once we get back to the inn."

He had called it the inn, not home. Molly prayed that didn't mean he'd decided to turn down Leah's offer and leave Lost Creek. That was exactly what it sounded like.

She clasped her hands together, whispering her silent prayers. Surely, the Lord would open Leah's eyes before she ruined the dreams she'd had for her nephew.

When they came to a stop in the driveway, Aaron thrust the reins in her hands, jumped down and took the bags into the house. Feeling like a coward, Molly was grateful that dealing with the horse and buggy had fallen to her. At least she'd have time to think while she did it. So far nothing had occurred to her, but a great idea was always possible, wasn't it?

No great ideas came. She turned Gus into the paddock, fastened the gate and walked reluctantly toward the house. She couldn't run away from this confrontation, not if it was remotely possible to stop Leah and Aaron from hurting each other.

She took the steps slowly, listening for the sound of raised voices. She could hear Leah saying something in a muted tone, perhaps trying to convince Aaron that he was wrong or Ruth Byler had misunderstood what she'd told her.

As soon as she heard Aaron's curt voice, she knew it hadn't worked. She went hurriedly into the house, praying softly for guidance.

The kitchen looked the same as ever...the slanting ray of sunshine turning the geraniums bright red still on the windowsills while the green sprouts of sweet basil looked as if they'd burst out of their pots. Unfortunately, the tension in the room didn't match the sunshine.

Leah, sitting at the kitchen table, gave her a look that would be pleading in anyone else, but Leah didn't plead. As for Aaron…he just glared at her and then turned back to his aunt.

"It was impossible to mistake the woman's meaning. She obviously thought that Molly and I…"

He couldn't seem to say anything else.

Molly sucked in a breath. "We met Ruth Byler in the coffee shop. You know how Ruth is. If an idea comes into her head, it comes out of her mouth."

Molly was rather pleased with that explanation. What she'd said was true, but it omitted whatever part Leah had played. And Leah had talked to her without a doubt. Ruth loved to pass on tidbits of information about people, but she wouldn't make something up.

Frowning, Aaron shook his head. "I should have known you had something in mind, Aunt Leah. I thought you understood my feelings. I married for life. Rachel was the only woman I could ever love."

It would be best if Leah said nothing at all in response to that, because almost anything would make it worse.

"You're a young man, Aaron, and you have a child who needs a mother. You don't see that now, but—"

"I told you quite clearly how I felt," Aaron interrupted her, his words like icicles dropping from his lips. "If you think I can't run the inn without a wife, you're wrong. And if that's a condition of your offer to me…" he paused, his expression bleak, "…we'll leave tomorrow."

Leah winced as his words struck her, and the pain in her eyes twisted Molly's heart. Leah had done just what he accused her of, but however right he was, another wrong didn't make a right.

"Aaron, don't." The words burst out of Molly. "Your aunt loves you."

He looked as if he didn't even hear what she said, just bursting out with an accusation aimed at her.

"If you are looking to replace your fiancé, you've come to the wrong man."

The temper Molly thought she had under perfect control suddenly burst like a fast-flowing river breaching a dam.

"How dare you!" She stamped her foot. "I'm not looking for a man to take care of me. I can take care of myself. And if I did, I for sure wouldn't consider anyone like you!"

The anger still roiled, but she clamped her lips closed on it. She would not say another thing to that impossible man. Silence hung between them, weighted with all the things they hadn't said.

It was broken by the sound of a sob.

Molly's breath caught. She turned toward Leah. Surely, Leah wouldn't...

No, she wouldn't. She hadn't. Leah was staring through the screen door to the porch. Becky stood there, tears pouring down her cheeks, her hands covering her ears, trying to shut out their words.

"Becky." She said the name and started forward, but Aaron nudged her ot of his way. He pushed the door open enough to scoop up his daughter, wrapping his arms around her and crooning soft words of comfort.

There was no comfort in the look he turned on her. *Stay away from my daughter.* It was as clear as if he had shouted it. He stamped out of the room with Becky, and neither she nor Leah could say a word.

Chapter Nine

The sound of a child crying seemed to go on and on. It subsided to muffled sobs for a few minutes, and Aaron's soft voice reached Molly where she stood at the top of the stairwell. She couldn't make out the words, but the tone was comforting.

It didn't seem to be helping. Becky sobbed as if her heart were broken. People were wrong when they said children were quick to forget. A broken heart hurt just as much at eight as it did at eighty. Poor Becky was distraught, and judging by Aaron's voice, he was, too.

He didn't want her, or his aunt. He blamed them, and she could understand that. But he had it wrong—he didn't understand. She, at least, hadn't had any part in Leah's matchmaking, and even Leah wanted nothing but good for Aaron and Becky. She just hadn't understood what that good would be.

The sobs started again, rising in a crescendo that battered Molly's ears. She couldn't take it any longer, and most likely Aaron would accept help from anyone at this point. She hoped so, at any rate.

Clutching the basin and towel she carried, she pushed the door to Becky's room open with her elbow and entered.

Becky sat on her bed, clutching her pillow against her with both arms. Her face was puffy and red, her cheeks stained by tears. The sight wrenched Molly's heart, seeming to wring it dry.

Aaron sat next to his child, his arm around her, a look of complete helplessness on his face. He looked at Molly, and she knew that whatever he'd said, he was desperate for help.

"Now, then," she said quietly as she walked toward them. "Becky, you're all hot and your throat hurts from crying, ain't so?" She tried to sound matter of fact, sure that was the best way to approach the child. "Let's see if we can do something about that." She sat down next to Becky, busying herself by wringing out a soft cloth in the cool water.

"Wh…what are you doing?" Becky got the words out in spite of the sobs, encouraging her. Molly moved closer, moving the cloth over Becky's forehead.

"Making you feel better," she answered. She smoothed the cool cloth over Becky's swollen eyes. "Is it working?"

Becky didn't move at first. Finally, she nodded her head. "A little bit." She hiccupped. "Just a little."

"That's good." She moved her arm across Becky's back, cradling Becky against her, her own arm resting on Aaron's. She wasn't looking at him, but she could feel the strong muscles that protected his child. "Let's keep it up, then."

Slowly, gently, she continued to bathe Becky's face, feeling the child relax, ever so slowly against her. If only Aaron didn't say anything too soon, hopefully that hysterical crying was over. He could be so impatient at times, though.

"You're feeling better, I know," she murmured. "Just rest." Child or adult, the aftermath of such prolonged weeping was to fall asleep, and that might be the best thing for Becky, once she'd been reassured.

She felt Aaron inhale, saw his lips move, and lightly pinched the arm underneath hers. At his indignant glance, she shook her head. Aaron jaw hardened, but he stayed quiet.

"You're okay now, Becky. You heard us arguing, and that scared you, didn't it?"

Becky's head moved in the slightest nod.

"We shouldn't have done that. Nothing is ever gained by raising your voice with someone. That's right, isn't it?" Again, the slight nod from Becky.

Molly might have imagined a faint flush in Aaron's face, but he seemed willing to let Molly carry on.

"I'm very sorry about it," Molly said, glancing at Aaron. Would Aaron take his cue? Now was the time for him to speak.

He caught her eye and then looked down at Becky. "I'm sorry, too." She felt as if he forced himself to say only that. Right now, this was about Becky, not about them.

"Do you think you could tell us what you're afraid of?" She held her breath, afraid to say more.

Becky clamped her lips together and seemed to struggle with herself. She flickered a glance up at her father. Whatever she saw seemed to reassure her, but her lips still trembled. Then the words burst out in a rush like a torrent of water gushing down the mountainside.

"I don't want to go away, Daadi. Please don't let's go away."

Aaron looked down at the woeful face and trembling lips, and she thought his own trembled for a moment.

"Becky, I promise I'll do everything I can so that we can stay."

Becky sagged against Molly, suddenly seeming boneless in the way a tired child does. "Good," she murmured. "Good."

Becky didn't catch the reservation in the words, but Molly did. He would do everything he felt he could do, but where would he draw that line?

Becky's breath grew slow and even. Her head was heavy on Molly's breast, and she was afraid to move until she could be sure not to wake her.

The silent moments crept on. Aaron's whisper reached her. "Sorry."

"We all are." She reached out with one hand to move the basin out of the way. "I think we can tuck her up on her bed for a nap, yah?"

He bent to look more closely at her face. Seeming satisfied, he moved, arranging the pillow, then took Becky in both arms to slip her into place. Molly drew the quilt around her and then put the soft doll on the pillow next to her and dropped a light kiss on Becky's forehead.

Moving softly, they exited the room. Aaron left the door ajar. They would hear if she made a sound, but Molly felt sure the crying was over.

Aaron started down the stairs with her behind him. Then abruptly, he stopped, turning. He was a step below her, making their faces on the same level. She thought he looked a little embarrassed. He cleared his throat.

"What I said before, about you wanting to..." The sentence died away, but they both knew he meant what he said about her engagement. "I must have sounded as conceited as a cock crowing on the fence. I didn't mean it."

"Yah, and I'm sorry for what I said. It was stupid." She could feel the flush warming her cheeks even as she smothered a laugh. "There's something about raising our voices that makes us say foolish things."

"I'm sorry," he began again, but she shook her head.

"No need to say it to me, but you have to understand. Your aunt…she just thinks what a perfect solution would be and tries to make it happen. Good for business, maybe, but not for people."

He nodded, but his face stiffened a bit. "I'll try to straighten it up with her. But I'm not getting married to please her."

"I know. And I'm sure she knows, too."

They went on down the steps and paused at the bottom. "I'll go work in the office for a bit while you talk to Leah."

For a moment, she thought he looked as if he'd ask for her help, but then he nodded and went on into the kitchen. She could only pray that they'd both be sensible. And loving.

Later, needing a little time alone after his challenging talk with his aunt, Aaron collected the toolbox that was stored in the pantry and headed for the barn. Doing something with his hands had always been a good way to set his mind to thinking. While his hands were busy with a routine task, he could mull over the situation with Aunt Leah and the inn.

He walked by the paddock, where Gus pricked up his ears and looked at him as if to ask him a question. Aaron shook his head. "Not now, Gus."

The horse dropped his head to the grass, for all the world as if he'd understood. Well, maybe he did. Animals that were around people a lot seemed to be able to put sounds and movements together to know what was going on.

This morning, he'd found Gus with his head between the stall bars, busily engaged in trying to knock the lid off the grain container. So Gus had to spend his time in the paddock until Aaron had a chance to fix it. If there was one thing horses were smart about, it was working their way into any available food. Too bad they weren't smart enough to know that gorging on grain could leave them plenty sick.

He took out the latch he'd bought and the screwdriver and set about detaching the old latch. As usual, the routine chore set his mind free to relive that talk with his aunt.

Aunt Leah insisted she hadn't meant to talk about her hopes for the future with the busiest busybody in the county. But lying there in the dark, tired of feeling helpless, the words had just come out. She should have known better. She knew as well as anyone that Ruth Byler couldn't resist knowing something no one else did—know it and spread it, embroidering it all the while.

Much as he was tempted to blame his aunt, he could understand. He'd had those long nights when he'd stared at the dark ceiling, going over and over his life with Rachel and longing for someone to talk to.

In the end, he'd accepted Aunt Leah's assurance that she'd just been wishing for the outcome that seemed so perfect to her—that the two people she loved best would come together. She'd promised there'd be no more matchmaking.

Now if only they could go back and stop the rumor before it got started…

The sound of buggy wheels outside diverted his attention. He reached the doorway to find Molly's brother Josh coming in with a heavy bag of feed over his shoulder.

"Delivery for you, Aaron," he said cheerfully.

"For me?" He stepped out of Josh's way and watched him empty the bag into the metal feed bin.

"You didn't know your aunt gets her feed from us?" Josh moved back, shaking out the bag. "She doesn't need much just for Gus and those few chickens, so Daad orders a little extra to supply her."

"Makes sense." Aaron fell into step with Josh. "Is there more?"

Josh nodded. "Two more bags. That's usually what fits in the bin unless Gus has been off his feed." He grinned. "And that never happens."

"For sure." Aaron grabbed one of the bags. "This morning, he was busy trying to break the stall door so he could get at the grain."

Working together, they emptied the rest of the bags. Josh leaned back against the partition once it was done, removing his hat to wipe his forehead and run a hand through rust-colored hair that was a bit darker than Molly's. For a moment, Aaron saw an image of Molly, smoothing her hair under her kapp, and he wondered how it would look streaming down over her shoulders.

He pushed that image out of his mind.

Josh stretched and nodded. "That's a gelding, all right. The older they get, the smarter they are. So how is everything going?"

Something about that casual question raised Aaron's hackles. "Have you been talking to your sister?"

Josh eyed him. "If you just mean talk, sure, we talk every day. Can't hardly help it. But if you mean gossip, that's not Molly's way."

"Sorry," he muttered. "Guess I'm too sensitive."

"Well, I did hear a bit of gossip about you and Molly. Has Leah been playing matchmaker?"

"What makes you say that?" he asked sharply.

"Hey, take it easy." Josh spread his hands wide. "I said I heard it, not that I believed it. As a matter of fact, my mamm was talking to Daad about it. And don't ask me how Mamm knows. Those women seem to hear everything that's going on. She said you and Molly ran into Ruth Byler when you were in town." He shook his head. "That woman wants to mind everyone's business."

"I hope folks know that about her." He moved uncomfortably, realizing he hadn't even thought about Molly's feelings. "I hope Molly's not too upset."

Josh grimaced, his open face worried for a moment. "Mamm will talk to her. That'll help. But it's not so easy after all the talk there'd been about her and Will."

A pang struck Aaron's heart. He should have thought of that. "It's worse for her than for me. I'm sorry about it."

"Yah." Josh's expression was clouded, and he looked very like Molly when she was worried about something. "I have to say that I never had such a desire to tackle somebody in my life as I did with Will. And he'd always been such a nice guy."

"Makes sense." Aaron wished he hadn't gone anywhere near this subject. "Your sister wouldn't have fallen for him otherwise."

"She's my sister, so maybe I'm prejudiced, but that's what I think." The clouds vanished, and Josh's smile returned. "Well, I should get going." He started toward the buggy and then stopped, shaking his head. "I'm forgetting one of the reasons I came over. Mamm says to tell Molly she's bringing Dorie over after supper so the little girls can have a quilting lesson. Is that okay?"

"Yah, sure, it's good of her. Becky will love it." And it was another thing that would bring him and Molly together.

He waved Josh off with their thanks for delivering the grain. There was no sense in thinking everyone was conspiring to bring him and Molly together. Her mother was doing something nice for Becky, not trying to trap him.

The supper dishes had made it as far as the sink before Leah sent Molly searching for the box of small quilt squares that would be perfect for doll quilts. Fortunately, the box was where Leah had thought it was, so Molly came hurrying downstairs with it when Becky called out excitedly they were here.

Molly plopped the box on the table and reached the back door in time to see her mother and Dorie drive up. "We're here! We're here!" Dorie jumped in her seat, waving both hands at Becky. Before Molly could reach her, Dorie had hopped down and run to hug Becky.

"We see you're here, Dorie." Molly reached up for the basket of quilting materials her mother was handing down. Her eyes met those of her mother, and they both smiled. "I don't think I want to be within range of Dorie's needle."

Dorie giggled. "Don't worry. I won't stick anybody. Except maybe me."

"I wouldn't be surprised," Molly answered, which both girls thought was very funny.

"Komm in, komm in," Leah called from the doorway. "We're all ready for you."

"Gut!" Dorie said. "And you know what?" She tugged at Molly's hand. "You know what, Molly?"

"No, tell me."

"Mammi and me left right after we ate, and David has to help Lida wash the dishes. Isn't that funny?"

"Not funny," Molly said. "Just fun. And everyone should know how to wash a dish in case they have to."

"David will be glad of it someday." Aaron had stepped up on the back porch in time to hear that.

Dorie looked skeptical, but she didn't argue. Instead, she turned to Becky. "What color do you want your quilt to be? I want mine to be bright."

Becky considered Dorie's question while they were getting settled at the kitchen table, which Leah was covering with small quilt patches of all colors. "I don't know. Something my dolly would like." She held up the doll as if to show her the fabric.

Aaron, probably thinking he should take an interest in the project, leaned on Becky's chair to look at the patches... some solid colors, some prints or stripes. "Your eyes are blue. What about some of the blue ones?"

Becky nodded vigorously. "Blue, yah."

Molly turned back to the sink while Leah was explaining the way a nine-patch quilt was laid out and Mammi brought patches together in different patterns.

Sure they'd spend most of their time arranging and rearranging the patches, Molly added more hot water to the sink and began washing dishes.

Aaron stopped behind her. "Don't you want to run over to the inn and let the machine do the washing?"

"Not a bit. I think I get them cleaner than any machine." She gave a little extra rub to the plate in her hand. No sooner had she rinsed the first few than Aaron reached across and began to dry.

Fearing his attempts would be like the eggs he dropped on the floor, she shook her head. "Don't bother. I'll take care of it."

"Aren't you the person who said that everyone should know how to do dishes?" The fine lines around his eyes crinkled.

"You already know, don't you?" She wished she hadn't asked the question almost as soon as it came out. It couldn't help but be a reminder of his own time of trying to be both mother and father to his child.

Sure enough, she saw the laugh lines vanish. But he just shrugged. "Yah, people learn when they have to, ain't so?"

Molly nodded. Aaron had had to, for sure. She thought of how inept she'd felt during her early days of working at the inn. Now, looking back, she couldn't imagine herself so lacking in confidence. She had changed and grown so much in the time since Will left. "When I started here, I was so afraid of making a mistake. But Leah just kept pushing me to do more than I thought I could."

"I guess that's her way." Aaron gave his aunt a long considering look, as if thinking of her attitude toward him by that scale.

Molly wanted to say something helpful, but before she could think of the right thing, her mother was calling her over. "Molly, come help Becky arrange her pieces. I'll warm up Leah's coffee for her."

She could interpret her mother's look at Leah. Leah's face was showing lines of tiredness. It wasn't surprising, given how active she'd been despite the casts she still had to wear. Molly scolded herself. She was as close to Leah as anyone, and she should have been more aware.

But as soon as Leah realized what they were doing, she

shook her head. "No, I don't want any more. And I'm not too tired for something that's so much fun as working with these sweet girls."

Molly knew her mother wanted to insist, but there'd be no talking Leah out of it now. The next time, she promised herself, she'd see that Leah had a good long rest before the quilting lesson.

She went back to the sink to find that Aaron had taken over the washing. She nudged him. "Can I have my job back?"

Aaron shook his head, giving her a teasing smile. "You've been demoted to drying."

"If you insist." She picked up the towel and the next dish in the rack. Amazing, that they'd been together this long and not found something to disagree about.

Automatically, she scanned the plate before starting to dry.

Aaron started to chuckle. "Ach, you're not going to start rewashing this the way you do with the ones from the dishwasher, are you?"

Molly tried to keep a straight face. "Are you sure I don't need to?"

"Positive." He reached over to tweak the end of the towel she held. "I'm better at it than any dishwasher."

"If you say so," she said, laughing. "I trust you."

In an instant, his face had sobered. "Do you?" he murmured. His gaze held hers for a long moment, and she couldn't seem to move.

The dish she'd been holding slipped. If not for Aaron's swift movement, it would have crashed to the floor. So much for her fear that he'd be the one to break something.

"Denke," she murmured, taking it back, focusing on the

plate so that she wouldn't get lost in his eyes again. She felt suddenly as if she hadn't been breathing and took a long breath.

Molly set the plate carefully on the counter. Those few minutes, she'd felt as if they were looking into each other's thoughts. But that couldn't happen. Even if she had felt free, Aaron had made it clear that he didn't and never would.

Chapter Ten

By the next afternoon, Molly had convinced herself that she'd been imagining things when it came to feelings about Aaron. This was helped along by the fact that he hadn't been around for most of the day—he'd been helping Daad and Josh put up a final load of hay in the morning and gone off to town this afternoon to take care of some business for Leah. They'd had supper without him, but she had a meal in the warming oven for him, in case he came home hungry.

The house felt empty at the moment, although Becky was upstairs doing homework while Molly tried to get Leah's wiry gray hair in order after her therapy session with Tim. "It looks like you were wrestling instead of exercising," she said. "How did your hair get involved in the exercises?"

"After the workout I had, I feel like I was wrestling." Leah stretched a bit and then rubbed her shoulder. "Tim was determined to get the last ounce of strength out of me today."

"Here, let me." She pushed Leah's hand gently out of the way and began massaging the sore shoulder. "He says you'll be getting the casts off soon. Then you'll be able to get around like your old self."

Leah didn't respond to Molly's attempt to cheer her up. "Not the way I feel right now."

"Now, Leah…" Molly began, but Leah shook her head, giving her a reluctant smile.

"Don't mind me. I'm a cranky old woman today. I thought that by this time I'd be able to take care of Becky and get back to normal instead of being useless."

"You're not useless," she declared. "You're the one who knows everything about the inn. And no one minds trying to fill in for you."

"I mind," Leah said tartly. "It's a gut thing you were planning to stay tonight. Who else would be ready to serve two suppers and take care of both Becky and me?"

Molly hesitated before attempting to reply. Leah really was out of sorts this afternoon, and Molly wasn't sure what had caused it. Was she still stewing about the failure of her matchmaking scheme?

She brushed the idea away. She didn't want to bring that up again, and she looked for a change of subject.

"Aaron is longer than I thought he'd be," she said, glancing at the clock. "Becky should be getting ready for bed before long."

"I thought he'd be late." Leah seemed happy that her forecast had been right. "I told you, didn't I?"

"Yah, you did." She put a last pin in Leah's hair. "How did you know?"

"He had to stop at the harness shop. I knew he couldn't resist the temptation to see how it's run." Seeing Molly's blank expression, she went on. "Didn't you know that's what he did before they came here? He managed a harness business."

Molly turned that over in her mind. "No, I didn't. I thought he'd worked construction. Didn't you tell me that?"

"That was before his wife died. After that, he had to do something that didn't mean traveling because he had to be with Becky."

"Yah, I see. But didn't he have any experience in the hotel business?"

Leah seemed to hear her unspoken criticism. "Managing is managing," she said, her voice tart. "Anyway, I knew he'd be all right with you and me both helping. But it didn't turn out that way, did it?" She smacked the arms of the wheelchair.

"He's doing a good job," Molly began, but Leah seemed to be preoccupied with her own troubles.

"I'm getting old, that's the trouble," she said, ignoring Molly's words. "The accident made me older than I should be. I've heard people say that it ages you, but I never thought it was true until now."

Fortunately, Becky came down the stairs from her room just then, so Molly didn't have to keep trying to reassure her. She hadn't done a very good job so far.

Becky was carrying her faceless rag doll clutched against her shoulder. "I still don't see Daadi coming," she said. "I looked out all the windows, and I don't see him anywhere." Her face puckered up a little. "He said he'd be home to tuck me in."

"Well, it's not time for that yet, is it?" Just now Molly thought that Becky's worries would be easier to deal with than Leah's. "Tell you what. Why don't we go get you ready for bed? We can get everything put away and then maybe play a game or tell some stories."

Becky brightened. "Will you tell me a real story about

something that happened when you were my age? I like real stories."

It was nice to see Becky speaking out about what she wanted. "If that's what you want, that's what we'll do. Tell Aunt Leah good-night, and we'll go up."

Becky hurried over to the wheelchair and then paused. "Can I give you a hug, Aunt Leah? I don't want to hurt you," she explained carefully.

That overture from Becky, who always seemed a bit in awe of her great-aunt, surprised all three of them. Leah's face warmed, all the grumpiness gone. She held out her arms. "You surely can, sweet girl."

Molly's heart swelled at this sign of acceptance on both their parts. Blinking back a tear, she held out her hand to Becky. They headed upstairs to Becky's room.

Once there, Becky darted to the window again. Then she turned back, shaking her head. "Why isn't Daadi here by now? I don't like to be in the dark without him."

Molly put her arm around the child, suddenly realizing what was on her mind. She must be afraid that something has happened to him. And if so, what will happen to her?

Her throat grew too tight to speak. She'd always been completely wrapped up with family—aunts and uncles, sisters and brothers, and a whole crowd of cousins. But little Becky was oddly bereft of relatives for an Amish child. Leah was her great-aunt, of course, but she was fairly old to take on an eight-year-old by herself. Looked at in that way, it wasn't surprising that Leah was so eager to find a wife for Aaron. But she'd have to convince him first.

"I promise you that Daadi will be here soon. He'll be pleased when he sees that you got ready for bed by yourself, ain't so?"

As if in answer, Becky marched to the chest and took out her nightgown. "Let's hurry. He has to be home by then or he won't be able to tuck me in. He always is. He wouldn't miss that."

Molly couldn't speak for a moment. Becky had faith in her father. She just hoped nothing would happen to disrupt that faith, at least not now.

It wasn't until Becky was ready to climb into bed that they heard the welcome thud of Gus's hooves and the creak of the buggy. Becky listened intently until she heard him speak, and then her smile blossomed like a flower.

"I said he'd be here in time. Didn't I say that?" She hopped onto the bed and bounced until she heard his steps on the stairs, then she slid quickly under her quilt.

"Daadi!" Becky held out her arms when he appeared in the doorway. "I said you'd be home to tuck me in. Didn't I, Molly?"

"You surely did." She smoothed the quilt around Becky. "Do you want Daadi to tell the story?"

Becky shook her head and patted the bed next to her. "Komm sit here, Daadi. Molly is going to tell me a really true story that happened to her."

Aaron had a smile for each of them as he sat down and put his arm around his daughter. "A really true story sounds wonderful. Go ahead, Molly."

Was he laughing at her? She wasn't sure, but she needed to tell a story that addressed Becky's fears, and she knew just what it would be. She settled herself comfortably against the headboard of the bed.

"This happened when I was about your age, and my bruder Joshua was two years younger. A bunch of Amish people went on a trip in a bus to Niagara Falls. That's a place where a river goes over a cliff and falls way, way down where it starts to flow along like any river again. It's very, very noisy, and there was a big crowd of people there and I started to feel a little bit scared because I'd never been in such a crowded place."

Becky scooted a little closer. "I would be scared, too."

"Mammi told me to stay close to her, but she had Joshua by one hand and my little cousin Mary by the other. So I had hold of her skirt and I wouldn't let go."

"Where was your daadi?" Becky's voice was hushed, and Molly began to wonder if this was such a good story, after all.

"He had to help Grossdaadi who was in a wheelchair like your Aunt Leah. So I held on tight. But then a bunch of new people got off a bus and crunched in around us and people pushed this way and that and everyone was talking Englisch. I lost hold of Mammi's skirt. I was scared, but I knew Mammi's skirt was dark blue, so that's what I looked for. And there it was. I grabbed the dark blue skirt and held on tight. Then I looked up, and you'll never guess what I saw. It was an Amish woman, all right, but it wasn't my mammi at all. It was someone I never saw before."

"What did you do?" Becky was caught up in the story, but she didn't seem afraid anymore.

"The lady bent down and talked to me in Deutsch. As soon as I heard that, I wasn't so afraid, and I told her what had happened and that I didn't know where my family was. And she said, 'Don't you know that all Amish people are brothers and sisters?' That was just like something my mammi would say. I nodded. And the lady's husband lifted me up above his head and said my name in a loud voice. Then I heard Mammi calling my name, and I knew it was okay."

Becky snuggled against her. "Is that really, really true that all Amish are brothers and sisters?"

"Really, really true," Molly said, and kissed her forehead lightly.

"So I'm like Dorie and David's sister."

She was obviously trying to wrap her mind around it.

"That's right. And if you need us, we will always be here."

Becky snuggled her doll close against her. "I like that," she said, her voice getting sleepy. "Do you like that, Daadi?"

Molly was almost afraid to look at Aaron, but when she did, he was smiling at her.

"Yah, I like that, too."

Aaron sat on Becky's bed until she fell asleep. He shouldn't have delayed in town so long. He should have realized that Becky wouldn't want to go to bed until he was here.

He considered that thought and wondered if it was just that or if he was missing something. He had seen the expression on her face when he'd come into the room. She wasn't just glad to see him. She'd looked relieved. Why?

Entering the kitchen, he found Molly setting out a steaming bowl of beef stew next to a fresh loaf of bread. He hadn't known he was hungry until that moment.

But satisfying his hunger would have to wait. He stood opposite to Molly with the table between them. "Becky was upset that I was late, ain't so?"

Molly and his aunt exchanged glances before Molly spoke. "Well, I think she was determined to stay awake until you got home."

"Upset," he said again. "I want to hear the truth, Molly. Don't bother to sugarcoat it."

Molly focused on pouring a mug of coffee for him. "I guess you could call it upset. Maybe she hadn't thought that you might be late."

"Ach, Molly, tell him the truth." Aunt Leah broke in. "Becky depends on you. We've tried to make her feel secure, but you're the heart of it. She can't feel safe without you."

"She will," Molly assured him, longing to take the bereft look from his face. "It will take time for her to know she can rely on us."

Aaron nodded and sank down into a chair. Molly promptly pushed the food in front of him. "Eat something. You can't solve problems on an empty stomach."

"That sounds like one of your mamm's sayings," his aunt commented. "She's always practical." She shook her head, but Molly just laughed.

"Someone has to be," she said. "Where would we be if none of us was practical?"

Aaron nodded, picking up a piece of fresh baked bread and spreading butter with a lavish hand. "All right, I get it. Without a mother, Becky depends a lot on me—maybe too much. That's what you're thinking, yah?"

"She's only eight." Molly's voice was gentle. "She'll learn to trust others besides you. It will just take time."

He caught her eyes. "That was the point of your story, ain't so?"

Molly nodded while Aunt Leah demanded to know what story.

"She told Becky about how she got separated from her family in a crowd, and some other Amish people rescued her," he said.

"Niagara Falls," Aunt Leah put in. "That's it, yah? I remember. Your mamm was fit to be tied."

"Of course, she was. And she felt guilty," Molly said. "I didn't realize that at the time, but she talked about it later." Molly's smile lit her face. "And she uses that story when she wants to emphasize that the young ones should hold onto a grown-up in a crowd. In fact, the whole family knows it by heart."

"It's not surprising," Aaron said, thinking of how he'd feel if Becky got lost in a crowd. Even worse than he did now, just because he'd been late. "Being a parent is a big job."

"Especially by yourself," Molly said quietly.

"It will get better," Leah said, but then a shadow crossed her face. "I hope it will, anyway. How would I know? Ask Molly."

The pain of her childlessness was written on her face after all these years. Aaron winced, wondering how much that had to do with her action in choosing him to take over the inn. He glanced at Molly, hoping she had something to say to get them out of this awkward corner.

"I should think it will just be different," Molly said. "I expect children will always make you worry, whether they're eight or eighteen." The look she gave him was filled with sympathy, and he thought again how kind she was.

"How did you get to know so much about it?" he asked. "Listening to your mamm?"

She nodded, chuckling a little. "And watching. Maybe it's because I'm the oldest. I got to watch Mamm and Daad bring up the rest."

He nodded, but he thought she was making light of it. She seemed to have a natural instinct for motherhood.

He turned away from that thought. If Rachel had lived… his Rachel would have understood Becky. They were so alike. Each time Becky smiled, he saw Rachel in that smile.

That gaping hole in his heart ached even more. He could never love anyone else the way he'd loved her. His aunt thought he should marry again and give Becky a mother. Molly already loved Becky, and Becky trusted her. Aunt Leah thought Molly was the perfect person, and maybe she was right. But Molly wouldn't marry him without love, and he didn't have it to give.

With their first full autumn weekend coming up, Molly had plenty to keep her busy. She was on the office phone the next day when Aaron came in, saying her name. She held up her hand to him and gestured toward the phone. He nodded, leaning against the doorjamb as if to distance himself from her call.

Molly focused on the caller, trying to ignore him but too aware that he was listening. That was appropriate, she reminded herself. He had a right to hear any business calls.

"That sounds great, Rose. It will be a full house this weekend, so I'll leave two large casseroles ready to go in the oven along with the brown-sugar bacon."

After a few more laughing exchanges, she hung up and turned to Aaron. "That was Rose McCauley. She's one of the Englisch women who come in to do Sunday mornings when we're at worship."

He moved closer to the desk, nodding. "Yah, Aunt Leah mentioned that you have someone." He frowned. "Do you think Aunt Leah will go to worship this week?"

"I hope so. I think it would be good for her." She hesitated, wondering if she should have left that decision to Aaron. "But it's not up to me," she added quickly.

The corners of his lips quirked. "We both know she'll make the decision, ain't so? But I was thinking we might take two buggies, and one of us could bring her home early if she gets too tired."

"Good idea. But you're right, she'll do the deciding," she said, smiling at the thought of Leah accepting anyone's orders.

Aaron's smile faded slowly, and it seemed to her that his gaze went inward. She felt herself stiffen in response, wondering what was wrong.

"I wanted to talk to you—" he broke off at the sound of a buggy outside. Molly leaned over to see out the window.

"It's Dorcas Bitler," she said, recognizing the caller. "And Jacob Unger is with her." Molly spun away from the window. "I can't imagine how they have time to go out visiting now. They're getting married next Thursday."

Catching Aaron's wrist, she tugged him after her. "Komm along and meet them. Dorcas has a small farm and orchard just down the road. Jacob owns a company that makes small metal parts for other companies."

Aaron undoubtedly wondered what she was so excited about, but Dorcas had always been a good friend and her three boys a delight. Folks thought she probably wouldn't marry again, but God had brought a surprising person into her life. And now they were on their way to forming a new family.

They reached the kitchen just as Leah reached the back door and pulled it open. Dorcas bent to hug Leah before coming to her, and Molly embraced her.

"It's lovely to see you. I thought you'd be too busy getting things ready for the wedding to go calling."

Dorcas's usually serene face had lost a little of its serenity. "Busy, yah, and every day it seems something new comes up. I always thought a second wedding would be easy." She sent a loving glance toward Jacob, and he put his arm around her waist.

"Not changing your mind, are you?" he teased, making Dorcas laugh.

Molly felt a tinge of jealousy at their obvious happiness and pulled herself back to business, introducing Aaron to everyone.

"It's gut you're all here," Jacob said, taking over like the businessman he was. "We need four bedrooms for next Wednesday for some unexpected guests. We know it's short notice, but if you can manage..."

Aaron glanced at her, as if asking her opinion, and she felt a surprising wave of togetherness. He really was treating her like a partner.

She nodded. "I don't see a problem. It will mean a quick turnaround, but we can do it."

"I'll give you a hand," Aaron said quickly. "No eggs involved, yah?"

Molly laughed, and then had to explain his efforts to help on his first weekend.

Dorcas and Jacob left once the arrangements were made for their guests, and Leah watched them for a moment from the window before going in search of her knitting. Holding her notes about the reservations, Molly had just turned to go back to the office when Aaron caught her wrist, his fingers wrapping around it warmly.

"I want to talk to you about something," he began, but

they were interrupted again. Becky and Dorie came racing across the backyard, followed by Lida, and Leah rolled her way back into the kitchen.

Molly smiled, pulling her wrist free. It was the second or third time Aaron had tried for a private conversation this afternoon, but that conversation seemed destined not to take place.

Becky and Dorie raced in the door, and it occurred to Molly that Becky was getting more like Dorie every day. She enjoyed seeing Becky so lively, but it was possible others might not. She could try to get Dorie to settle down, but that never had worked very well.

Lida, coming more slowly after the girls, walked straight to Molly. "Mammi says to tell you that she'll come over in about an hour to do some more quilting with the girls. If that's not okay, I'm to take Dorie back with me."

Since both of the little girls were jabbering away to Leah, who was laughing and talking with them, she guessed it would be fine, especially since Leah laid aside her knitting and rolled her chair over to the cabinet that housed her quilting projects.

"Looks fine to me. Tell Mammi so."

Lida nodded, then put her arm around Molly's waist and drew her away from the others. "One other thing you have to know. Will is back."

She stiffened at the sound of the words. "Are you sure? This isn't just Sally being excited?"

"I'm sure," Lida said grimly. "He came today to pick up Sally. And I heard him myself saying how happy he was to be home again. He also said he was looking forward to seeing everyone on Sunday at worship."

"Well, I knew it was going to happen." She'd told herself a hundred times that it wouldn't bother her, but now that it was here, she felt as if she'd been tossed in the air and didn't know where she'd land. William was home, and apparently happy. What did that say to her?

Lida's arm tightened around her. "Are you okay?"

"Of course." Her voice was sharp, and she was instantly embarrassed. Lida was being helpful. She didn't deserve that.

"Sorry. That was stupid. I'm all right, but it's just a shock." Why was it a shock? She'd known he was likely to return. She'd heard it from his mother and his sister. She should have been ready.

Lida shook her head. "I'm the one to be sorry. I just thought you'd best hear it from me before you did from someone else. Or worse, ran into him."

"You're exactly right. Denke, Lida." Her little sister was being unexpectedly mature.

So, Will was planning to be at worship on Sunday. He must have already talked to the bishop, then. He'd be forgiven by the Leit, but Molly had to be sure she'd forgiven him. She couldn't sit in worship with anger in her heart.

"I guess I better get on home, or Mammi will wonder what's going on." Lida took a step or two, looked back, shook her head and went out quickly.

Molly glanced around. Leah and the children were still chatting away, but Aaron had come closer to her. Aaron must have heard at least part of their conversation.

"Sorry," he said, looking embarrassed. "I didn't intend to eavesdrop. I was just going to thank Lida."

"It doesn't matter. Everyone will know on Sunday." The whole Leit would witness their meeting. She cringed inside at the thought.

"You could stay home," he offered. "That way they'd be used to it by the next worship."

Molly shook her head, wishing she could put her hands over her ears and run out of the house. But she couldn't. She had a job to do, and a life to live. If only she could be sure of getting through it without falling apart.

Chapter Eleven

For a moment longer, Molly seemed to feel Aaron's questioning gaze on her face. Then he abruptly turned away, murmuring something about work to do, and vanished back into the inn. Relieved, she blinked away a tear that threatened to overflow and forced herself to push Will's return to the back of her mind.

Leah and the kinder were still talking about their project. Putting a smile on her face, she went to join them. A nine-patch doll quilt was one of those projects most often picked for a starting quilter—that, or a simple potholder. But Dorie had been determined on a quilt of some sort, and Becky had followed her lead, so the potholder suggestion had been dismissed.

Molly stretched over the back of Becky's chair to investigate. At the first session, they'd laid out the squares they wanted to use, but to no one's surprise, Dorie wanted to change the arrangement entirely. Fearing they'd linger at this stage and never get started, Molly moved over next to her little sister.

"Why would you want to do that? The orange and yellow look very nice together. Sort of sunshiny."

"Yah, but a quilt should make you want to go to sleep, ain't so? Maybe different shades of blue would be better."

Leah, who'd been studying Molly's face, chimed in on Dorie's side. "That's true. Dorie, you come over here and I'll help you pick while Molly helps Becky."

Judging from Leah's expression, she'd figured out that something was wrong. She probably thought Becky would be easier to deal with, and there was no doubt she was right. Released from the likelihood of an argument with Dorie, Molly scooted over to the seat next to Becky.

"You don't want to change yours, do you?" she asked cautiously.

Becky shook her head. "I like these colors." She put her finger on a light purple square next to the darker blue. "It makes me think of lilacs. We used to have a big lilac bush at home."

It was the first time Molly could remember that Becky had sounded a little homesick. Impulsively, she put her arm around the child. "We have a whole hedge of lilac bushes at our house—you'll see them blooming in the spring. Maybe we could plant one here for you."

Becky glanced at Leah, as if wondering what she'd think of the idea. Then she leaned back on Molly's comforting arm. "I'd like that," she whispered, smiling.

"Me, too," Molly whispered back. That confiding smile seemed to ease away some of the tension that lingered since she'd talked to Lida. After all, she had a good life without Will, and she'd gained so much confidence and independence since he'd gone out of her life. She could handle his return.

The sound of male voices in the backyard startled her so much that she ran a pin into her finger instead of the fabric.

But it wasn't Will—of course not. Aaron and David crossed the porch and swung open the screen door.

"Look who I found," Aaron said, putting his hand on David's shoulder.

Dorie wrinkled her nose. "I told you this was just for girls. We're making doll quilts. You don't want to do that, do you?" For a moment, she looked as if she were afraid of his answer.

"I thought maybe you'd be done by now." He came to lean over her shoulder. "What will that be?"

"I told you. A doll quilt."

"A nine-patch quilt," Molly suspected if she didn't intervene, the quilting project would fizzle out. "You see? Each of them has nine patches, and they're deciding on the best arrangement for them."

She glanced at Aaron, and he moved toward them as if answering her unspoken plea.

"I could use some help with the gate into the paddock, David. Want to help me?"

David nodded, abandoning the quilting without regret, and the two of them headed out the back door.

Maybe it was about the time when twins would develop different interests, Molly thought, wondering if she should mention this to her mother. But Mamm was probably well ahead of her by now.

Was she also ahead of Molly on the subject of Will's return? Most likely. Lida would have told her if no one else had. For a moment, Aaron's suggestion that she stay home on Sunday resounded in her ears. He'd been right in thinking that another two weeks would give people time to become excited about something else.

She couldn't. It would be cowardly. But she was grate-

ful to Aaron, even so. He'd shown an unexpected interest
and tried to help. Even a few days ago, he wouldn't have
bothered. She hadn't even thanked him. Maybe when her
mother showed up, she'd have an opportunity to do so.

A quick glance out the screen door showed her Aaron
smiling down at her little brother, demonstrating something about the gate latch. His relaxed expression touched
her heart.

Aaron could sense the tension as he drove the buggy to
the Miller farm for worship Sunday morning. Even Becky
seemed to have picked up on the atmosphere, and she snuggled close against his side as he drove.

Aunt Leah had rejected the idea of taking two buggies to worship in case she needed to come home early,
so here they were—unusually quiet. Aaron glanced sideways at Molly's face, but it told him nothing. She stared
at the changing colors on the side of the road, not meeting
anyone's gaze.

They'd been so busy with guests since Friday that he'd
had little time to reflect on Molly's feelings. In fact, she'd
managed to hide them successfully, until this morning.
Now she was clearly unable to think about anything other
than meeting with the man who had run away rather than
marry her—and in front of the entire congregation.

There was no reason for him to feel responsible, he told
himself. After all, this would be happening whether he had
come to Lost Creek or not. Unfortunately, that didn't make
him feel any better.

Well, the line of buggies had begun turning into the lane
at the Miller farm. The moment had arrived. The oldest
of the Miller boys came running, gesturing to him to pull

the buggy up just outside the large building that normally housed the machine shop.

"My daad says for us to get Leah settled inside, and then I'll take care of the horse and buggy." His blue eyes widened as he took in the wheelchair jammed into the back of the buggy.

"Denke, Thomas." Molly managed to sound normal as she slid down. "We'll get the chair out first."

By that time, Aaron was grasping the wheelchair, and the boy, Thomas, rushed to help him. There was an apron of concrete around the prefab building, so they wouldn't have to trundle the chair across rough ground.

It was a matter of a few minutes to have his aunt settled inside. To his relief, she no longer seemed apprehensive about being out. In fact, she looked around eagerly. Molly started to sit down next to her, but she waved her away.

"Go on outside and greet folks. No need for you to skip ahead of the line. I'm fine."

Molly looked as if she'd rather stay put, but his aunt didn't seem to realize it. He couldn't blame Molly—she'd already been the target of glances, some curious, some sympathetic.

Outside, folks were already gathering—men in one line, women in another. Becky darted over to Molly and grasped her hand. She waved at him, but she didn't seem in any doubt about where she belonged.

He glanced at Molly in amusement, only to find that her face was frozen, her eyes staring. Following the direction of her gaze, he spotted a young man he hadn't seen before. Judging by Molly's frigid stare, this must be Will.

He wasn't the only one to have noticed Molly's expression. He saw one woman nudge another, whispering. With an instinctive need to protect Molly from giving herself away, he took a few quick strides to stand in front of her, turning his back toward the onlookers. Molly blinked, focusing on his face.

"You don't want to give people reason to talk," he murmured.

"No...no." A flush came up in her cheeks. "I don't need help."

"Sorry," he snapped. So that's what he got for trying to help. A quick brush-off.

Clutching Becky's hand, she vanished inside, and through the open door he could see her and Becky settling on a bench next to his aunt's chair. Someone touched his arm, and Aaron turned to find Molly's father.

"Komm. You might as well sit with us, yah?"

Nodding, he walked with Caleb over to the men's line.

Caleb cleared his throat. "Molly...she's gotten so independent since she's been working at the inn. Wants to deal with everything by herself." He sounded as if he regretted that.

Defensive when it came to his aunt, Aaron tamped down a gust of annoyance. "I'm sure Aunt Leah didn't intend—"

"Ach, I didn't mean that." Caleb rushed into speech. "Leah has been wonderful kind to our Molly. But fathers always want to protect their daughters, ain't so?"

Aaron's irritation dissolved. "Yah, that's for sure." He glanced toward the door, but folks were starting to go in, hiding them from his gaze. And then they were moving, and he found himself shaking hands with the ministers and the bishop, then following Caleb to a bench on the men's side.

Now it was his opportunity to get a close look at Will. Good-looking, he guessed. At least the girls would think so. He looked younger than Aaron expected, with his light hair in an Englisch cut and a lively face that seemed ready to crinkle into laughter at the slightest excuse. *Englisch-looking*, he thought. So why didn't he stay out there in the world, instead of coming back to cause problems for Molly. He'd think the boy had enough sense to know better.

Will slid into a bench and sat, and Aaron decided he'd best stop staring at him before he was the one attracting attention.

The vorsinger began the long slow line of the first hymn, and Aaron let his gaze slip to Molly once again. Her lips moved with the words, but her eyes were fixed on the floor. At least she had a respite from curious stares and gossip during the service. Maybe by then Aunt Leah would be ready to leave. She'd probably want to get home in time to bid goodbye to their guests.

But by the time the service was over, Leah was surrounded by people who were happy to see her out, she was beaming as if she'd never heard of being tired.

And things looked much the same with Molly. While Will had a cluster of guys around him, Molly seemed busy with her own friends. Apparently, nobody needed him. Even Becky went running to Molly, grasping her hand. Molly's attention went immediately to Becky, and she bent to listen to her. The love that Molly had for her was obvious even from this distance, and his heart warmed at the sight. He'd tried to ignore his aunt's attempts at matchmaking, but he had to admit she was right about one thing. Molly loved Becky already, and Becky felt the same way. For the first time since his Rachel died, he thought seriously about marrying again. Not loving again. He could never feel about anyone the way he had about Rachel.

He found he was considering his aunt's matchmaking seriously. Perhaps Molly felt the same about Will as he did about Rachel. Was it possible she might think about marrying for other reasons than love? If she did, maybe it was time for him to think about the whole marriage question in a new light.

Molly was safely surrounded by friends, but she didn't really take much comfort in it—they were all being too careful. They carefully didn't look toward Will. Some of them were trying to shield her from the sight of him, while others chattered incessantly, probably hoping to distract her. She appreciated it, but she wanted nothing so much as to leave.

The benches from worship were carried out under the trees and flipped open to form tables, and the Miller girls and all their female relations hustled about, bringing food from the kitchen. Maybe Leah wouldn't find that comfortable, and they could leave early. She should go ask her.

She was about to move when the crowd shifted a bit and she had a clear view of Will. Before she could look away, he had nearly collided with Mattie Miller, who was carrying a tray of sandwiches. He made a grab, steadying the tray, saying something to Mattie with a laughing, teasing look.

It seemed no time at all since he'd been teasing her, smiling at her. Molly jerked her head around, managing to smile down at Becky and swing their linked hands.

"Why don't you go find Dorie and David? I'd guess they're looking at the baby goats." They walked together toward the small barn, which housed the goats.

"Are they really babies?" Becky asked, skipping to keep up with her.

"Well, not really, I guess, but they're smaller than regular goats are. They're called American Pygmy goats, and the Miller family raises them. I think they're very cute."

"Some people drink goat milk." She wrinkled up her nose. "I tried it once, but I didn't like it."

"Me, neither." Molly smiled at her expression, and the last of her tension slid away. "Goat cheese is good, though."

They went through the open door and found Dorie and David by the goat pen. Well, David was by it. Dorie had climbed up to the second rail and looked as if she intended to hop over the top one.

"Dorie!"

With a quick glance, Dorie hopped down, looking very innocent as she ran to grab Becky's hand. "Come see the goats, Becky. Aren't they cute?"

Molly followed them to the pen's gate. The curious goats, used to admiration, poked their heads through the bars. Naturally, Dorie put her hand through from the other side, and Molly pulled it back before the other two could copy her.

"Careful. They might think your fingers are carrots and take a bite."

"I wish we had carrots. Next time, I'll ask Mammi if we can bring some."

"You do that," Molly said, knowing that she'd long since have forgotten by the time they had worship at the Miller place again. "I think you'd best scoot out of here now. I need to check on Leah. You go see if Mammi wants help. You, too, Becky. All right?"

They nodded, and she watched them run off with linked hands.

Leah was sitting just inside the door, looking out at the

crowd bustling around, getting lunch ready. She looked up and smiled when she saw Molly.

"What happened to your crowd?" Molly asked. "Did they run out of gossip?"

Leah laughed. "What a thing to say! You must know they never do that. They dashed off to help with lunch." She stared down at her legs, the amusement gone from her face. "Ach, I'm so tired of sitting and watching other people do things. I want to get back to doing, too."

She said it lightly, but Molly could see the frustration in her eyes.

"You've never been one to sit, ain't so?" Molly patted her shoulder. "You remember what the doctor said—every step forward is a gut thing. And look at you. You're out to worship today. A week or two ago, you couldn't even think of that."

Leah reached up to clasp Molly's hand where it rested on her shoulder. "Yah, you're right. I'm being ungrateful, and after listening to a sermon on gratitude for the Lord's blessings."

"I'm sure He understands." Some people could stand being immobilized, but not Leah.

Leah chuckled. "I surely hope so."

"Do you want to get started home soon? If not, I'm sure we can get you over to the table."

"Ach, no. I have to say I'm ready to be back home. Maybe it's time for a nap."

"I'll go find Aaron, then," Molly said quickly, relieved that Leah was willing to admit when she'd had enough. Aaron had been over by the milking shed a few minutes ago. She darted around a corner and nearly ran into Will coming the other way.

Her stomach jumped, and she couldn't seem to find a word to say. Was he looking for her? She hoped not.

"Wilkom back, Will." She tried to sound as if she meant it.

"Denke, Molly. You're just the person I wanted to talk to…"

"Not here," she said quickly. Didn't he realize everyone would be looking at them? "Leah is ready to go home, and I must find Aaron to get the buggy ready."

"You can spare a minute for me, can't you? We have to talk sometime. Why not now?" He gave her the smile that usually had girls agreeing with whatever he said. She told herself it didn't work on her any longer. Why didn't he accept what she'd said?

"Not now," she said. "Some other time." She forced herself to sound firm.

"When? Come on, Molly. Please."

"I don't know." She took a step back. "Sometime."

"Molly, when? We have to talk. I have to tell you…"

But she couldn't deal with this right now. Turning, she scurried away, and the next minute she spotted Aaron coming in her direction. She felt a surge of relief.

Molly saw the way Aaron focused on her. Then the next moment, he was watching Will heading in the other direction. He reached her, but to her relief he didn't ask questions.

She rushed into speech before he could. "You aunt is ready to leave. I was just looking for you."

"I thought she'd come to it soon. I'll get the boys to bring the buggy over to the barn. We'll be right there." Aaron paused for a moment, as if words hesitated on his lips. Then he headed toward the buggy parking.

Molly found Becky with the twins and shook her head

at their pleas for a little more time. "Not just now. Leah is getting tired."

Becky grasped her hand and waved goodbye to the twins, and Molly suspected she was a little tired, too. It had been an early morning and a long service. Becky was probably ready for some quiet time, unlike Molly's little sister. Dorie would go on until she fell asleep where she stood.

It didn't take more than a few minutes for the boys who were acting as hostlers today to bring the buggy around the side of the building. By the time she was back with Becky, Aaron was lifting his aunt into the buggy seat. Becky scrambled in beside her, and Molly spread the lap robe over both of them.

Seeing that Leah was ready to leave, folks deserted the tables to come and say goodbye, and the oldest of the Miller girls handed up a basket filled with a little of everything for lunch, and waved away their thanks.

"Wonderful gut to see Leah today. Mammi says to enjoy the lunch."

Molly waved to her. When she turned to the buggy, she found Aaron holding out his hand to help her. His fingers closed warmly around hers. "Okay?" he said softly.

She nodded, grateful for his firm clasp and also for his tact. Aaron didn't laugh or tease or demand answers. He was just there. And she was glad.

Their eyes locked as he helped her up to the seat, and she felt as if a wave of caring and comforting passed between them. Then Aaron clucked to the horse, and they moved slowly toward the lane.

Chapter Twelve

Molly was pleased to find their guests still lingering at the inn when they returned, and Rose McCauley talking in an animated manner to the women guests. Then she saw Leah's tired face, and wished all were quiet so that Leah could slip away to bed. But Leah brightened up immediately, seeming delighted that she'd arrived in time to talk with their guests.

Aaron, heading back outside after helping his aunt, paused for a low-voiced comment to Molly. "Try to get her to take a rest, won't you?"

"I'll do my best." In her opinion, they could all use a nice nap.

Perhaps the guests realized that, at least as far as Leah was concerned. With a final round of goodbyes and promises to come again, they were off.

Leah leaned back in the wheelchair and closed her eyes for a moment. "You don't need to remind me, Molly, dear. I'm ready for a rest. That's what you're thinking, isn't it?"

Molly laughed. "Yah, it is. Mammi always sits back in her chair for a little nap after worship. I'll give you a hand getting settled. Will you have some lunch first?"

Leah shook her head. "Later," she said.

Leah fell asleep while Molly was pulling a coverlet over

her. Smiling, Molly tucked it in and tiptoed away. It was unusual to see Leah give in to tiredness, but Molly was relieved. Maybe Leah, determined as she was, had begun to realize her age at last.

Molly returned to the kitchen to find Aaron and Becky seated at the table, enjoying the basket that had come home with them. But Rose, who was usually gone by this time, was standing at the sink washing dishes. Molly picked up a dish cloth and nudged Rose.

"Are you trying to take away my job?" she teased. "Or are you just curious?" Then she caught the startled look on Becky's face and wondered what she was thinking.

"Neither one," Rose said. "I got too involved in talking with that nice bunch of guests. Besides, with Leah just getting back to worship today, I thought things might be extra busy."

Becky carried her plate over to the sink carefully, handing it to Rose, who took it with a quick smile. "Thank you, Miss Becky. That's nice of you."

With a quick glance at Molly, Becky spoke up. "Nobody could take over Molly's job." She looked embarrassed for a moment, but she didn't back down.

Rose chuckled. "Everyone knows that. She does it better than anyone, right?"

Becky nodded, and her lips curved in a sweet smile. "Right."

Molly had a feeling that Becky had surprised her father. Aaron paused for a moment, then held out his hand to Becky. "How about a nap for you, as well as for Aunt Leah?"

"I'm too old for a nap," she said, and then punctuated the words with a yawn.

Molly tried hard not to laugh. "Maybe reading for a bit, then."

"Good idea," Aaron said. "I'll go up with you, yah?"

Becky nodded. Swinging their clasped hands between them, they headed for the stairs.

Rose dried her hands. "She's really attached to her daddy, isn't she?" She picked up a stack of plates and started putting them away. "That's sweet to see. It's a challenge for a man to raise a child alone."

Molly nodded, wondering what was on Rose's mind. She had some reason for sticking around this afternoon, that was certain sure. "Is that the reason you stayed? To check on Becky and her daadi? Or have you heard a few rumors going around?"

"You know I never listen to rumors," she said, trying without success to look offended. Then she giggled. "Everyone's been asking me what's going on here. They think I've got a direct line to you. And besides, they're saying that your old boyfriend has come back home."

"I never doubted everyone in the Leit would know that, but how did the Englisch community get onto it?"

"My husband heard it at the hardware store, where else?" Rose leaned back against the counter. "And men say that they never gossip. What a story that is."

"You'd think they'd have better things to think about."

"Right." Rose squeezed her arm. "Now come on, tell me everything. Did he come back to marry you?"

"No, of course not." At least, she didn't think so. "That's silly."

"Why silly? Maybe he had a change of heart after all this time. Or maybe he left it too long, and you found someone else."

Rose was as hard to turn off and Hilda was. "Nothing like that. I'm just a different person now than I was then. Why can't anybody understand that?"

Rose lifted her eyebrows. "Sounds to me like you're protesting too much. Aaron seems like a nice person, is he?"

"Aaron has nothing to do with it. And neither does Will. I'm not looking for a husband," she said firmly.

"That doesn't mean one isn't looking for you," Rose said lightly. "Okay, I'll stop bugging you." She started toward the door, and then paused to look back. "But don't try to kid yourself, that's all. That never works." Laughing, she disappeared out the door.

Molly leaned against the sink, letting out a long breath. She hadn't been expecting that from Rose, but it wasn't really so surprising. They'd been friends as long as she'd been working at the inn, and they'd hit it off well right away. If Rose was sensing something in her, she just might be right.

She might be able to put Rose's comments out of her mind, but she couldn't block out Will. What did he want? Why had he come back? And what did he want to talk to her about?

Aaron heard the women's voices dying away as he and Becky went up the stairs. Apparently, Molly had friends everywhere in Lost Creek, Englisch as well as Amish. Would he and Becky ever reach that point? He doubted it. Molly had a natural gift for friendliness, and that was something that had been left out of his makeup. So Becky couldn't very well get it from him.

Meanwhile, Becky was marching up the steps as if trying to persuade him she was not sleepy, but he thought she'd be just as happy to relax with a book for an hour or so.

That might give him a chance to talk to Molly in private. He'd had a feeling, when he saw Will looking after Molly, that his approach hadn't been at a good time. Maybe he should have apologized and backed off...

Still, Molly hadn't looked as if she had any desire to talk to her former fiancé. And besides, it wasn't his business, was it, to try and bring them together?

He realized he'd come to a stop on the steps, and Becky had begun to tug on his hand. "I'm coming, I'm coming." He pushed away the other thoughts that crowded his mind. "Do you want me to read to you for a time?"

"Yah, denke." She skipped up the next step. "Let's start one of the *Little House* books. Molly says they were always her favorite books."

"Good idea," he agreed, thinking that Molly was having a profound impact on his little girl. They had slipped into each other's lives as if they'd always belonged there. That made it doubly hard to push Molly out of his mind.

They reached her room, and Becky tugged him toward the rocking chair by the window. "You sit there," she said, bossing him a bit. "I'll get the book."

Agreeably, he settled himself in the rocker. The window beyond the plain white curtains showed a patchwork of colors: orange, russet, brown, yellow, all contrasting and blending in a kind of colorful quilt showing off God's handiwork.

Becky came back with *The Little House in the Big Woods* and scrambled onto his lap. "Start at the very beginning and don't skip any," she directed. It occurred to him she was beginning to sound like Molly's little sister.

And more like the child she'd been before her mother passed. That would have made her mother happy. She'd never have wanted Becky to become so shy, but he couldn't seem to find out how to stop it. He blinked, wondering how many mistakes he'd made.

Becky wiggled and looked up into his face. "Are you thinking about something?"

"Not exactly." Realizing there was something on her mind, he focused on her face. "Are you?"

"No. Well, maybe." She stared down at her lap. "What Molly and her friends were saying before... Nobody's going to take Molly's job away from her, are they?"

"What would make you think that? You know that Rose and Molly were just kidding, don't you?" He stroked her hair back from her face.

She nodded, not looking at him. "I guess. Anyway, that's what they said. I just wanted to be sure."

"You can be absolutely sure." Nobody would replace Molly—at least, not unless Molly decided to leave.

Now Becky did look at him, and her small face lit with a smile. "That's good. I love Molly." For a moment, she looked a bit surprised at what she'd said, but then she gave a nod, as if reassuring herself.

Aaron focused on the story, but his child's words kept repeating in his thoughts. She loved Molly? Had she told Molly about her feelings?

But why should he be surprised? Everybody loved Molly, including Aunt Leah. After all, hadn't Aunt Leah been trying to push the two of them together? *Matchmaking...* The very word made him cringe. His aunt thought that he needed a wife and that Becky needed a mother. She'd thought Molly was the perfect solution.

He rubbed his fingers across his forehead. But he couldn't love anyone else—not the way he'd loved his wife. And as far as he could see, Molly couldn't love anyone else the way she'd loved Will. So why on earth was he thinking about it again?

He knew the answer to that question. Because he'd assumed that Becky felt as he did—that no one could replace Becky's mother. Now, with Becky declaring she loved Molly, maybe it was time to think that through again. Maybe being in love wasn't the only good reason to get married.

Molly finished cleaning up the kitchen and took a peek into Leah's room to find her sound asleep. Easing her way back out, she closed the door and slipped around to the office. She wouldn't work on Sunday, but she had left her knitting on the desk. That was a good thing to occupy her on a quiet afternoon, but she had no sooner settled in the kitchen rocking chair than she realized that knitting would give her too much time to think.

She forced herself to focus on the knitted caps she was making. Starting them in the early fall guaranteed she'd have quite a few done by the time cold weather came. And since they were made for charity, they could use a variety of colors. The variegated wool in different shades of blue pleased the eye and certain sure ought to keep her from letting her mind stray.

Molly tried. She really did. Her hands dropped in her lap. She could not keep from going back to those moments when she'd walked right into Will.

At least not many people had been looking their way at that moment. That was the only consolation. She didn't know what her expression had been, and she didn't want to know. As for his declaration that they had to talk… Well, they didn't. There wasn't any "they" any longer. When Will ran away from their wedding, he had ended that irrevocably.

The back door squeaked, as if to punctuate the word, and she looked up to find her mother coming in the door. Making a shushing gesture, she hurried to hug her.

"Everyone's napping," she said softly.

"Everyone?"

Molly chuckled softly. "Well, I know Leah is, because I just checked on her a few minutes ago. And Aaron took Becky upstairs to settle down with a book for a bit. He might have dozed off, too."

Mammi nodded, taking the chair next to her. "Like your daadi sleeping behind his newspaper."

"Just about." Daadi always insisted he was reading, but they were convinced he did it with his eyes shut. "Anyway, what brought you over this afternoon?"

Mammi nodded toward the door to Leah's room. "I thought she was tiring herself out. The first time back to worship had to be a struggle. I thought maybe I could convince her to rest."

If that was all that had brought her here, Molly would be very surprised. "Komm now. You wanted to hear how it went with Will."

She got the words out lightly, but her voice had begun to wobble at the end. Her mother clasped her hand comfortingly.

Molly blinked several times, and pressed her lips close together.

"Ach, my dear girl, the first time you saw each other was bound to be difficult. Next time it will be easier."

"I hope, but I don't want it to be soon." She took a deep breath. "But Will says he wants to talk to me. By myself.

I told him no, but you know how Will is. He won't take no for an answer."

Mammi gave a short nod. "He always thinks he can talk people into doing what he wants. It sounds as if that hasn't gotten knocked out of him yet. That's one thing I thought the outside world might do for him."

"I'm afraid not." No, he was the same Will, and that had good and bad sides. "I'm not upset about his coming back. I'd just like to ignore him until people stop talking."

Mammi was quiet for a moment, her gaze studying Molly's face intently. "Do you think…" She let the words slip away, as if not sure she should offer any advice.

Now it was Molly's turn to clasp her mother's hand. "It's all right. Really. If you want to tell me something that might help, please tell me." She pressed her lips together again, afraid they'd quiver.

"Yah, all right." Their hands grasped tightly, and her mother's eyes were filled with sympathy. "I wonder if it might be better to get together with him soon. I know you, Molly. The longer you wait, the more you won't want to do it. Better to do it soon and have it done with. Ain't so?"

For a moment, Molly stared at her mother and let the words sink in. A smile began to tug at her lips and the more she tried to suppress it, the more it grew.

Footsteps sounded on the stairs, and Aaron came round the doorframe into the kitchen. He looked at them, his gaze moving from one to the other. "Are you having a staring contest?"

Molly's laugh burst out. "Not exactly. Mammi was just proving that she knows me better than I know myself."

Mammi patted her hand. "Not everything. Just some things." Her mother stood up as Leah's bell rang.

"I'll go in and help her. Why don't you put on the kettle." She smiled. "It was wonderful gut to see her back in worship today. And even William, too."

Molly started toward the stove, but before she reached it, Aaron had intercepted her, putting a hand on her arm.

"Is that what you're thinking, too? That it was good to see William back?"

She wished her thoughts would stop whirling around. Or that people would stop asking her difficult questions.

Trying to plant a smile on her face, Molly looked up at him. "I'm not as far along on my Christian charity as my mother is."

Somehow, halfway through that sentence, she met Aaron's eyes, and the flippancy left her voice. Aaron was asking because he cared about things that were troubling her.

"Denke, Aaron," she added softly, hoping he understood the things she didn't say.

He nodded. "I was afraid I might have interrupted you when you and he were talking."

"I was glad to be interrupted." She lifted the kettle and set it on the gas burner, turning it on. "But my mother said that I may as well talk to him, because if I don't, it will just keep bothering me."

"Well, I don't want to run counter to your mother's advice. But I can understand not wanting to have a talk with him with the whole Leit around. I surely wouldn't."

For a moment, he seemed about to say something else, and he stood with his hand resting warmly on her arm. Her breath caught, and she couldn't look away. But then he turned and walked quickly outside, leaving her feeling as if a support had been pulled away.

Chapter Thirteen

Molly started off to work early on Monday morning. Lida had spent the night with Leah last night—the first time she'd done so. Molly suspected Mammi would never have agreed to that when she was Lida's age. Maybe by the time Mammi had gotten to her third child, she'd started to trust a little more. Or maybe Lida was more mature than she had been at that age. She'd hate to think that were true.

When she reached the lane, Molly paused for a moment to gaze up at the ridge that swept up from the river valley. It was clear enough this morning that she could see the shadowed outline of the next ridge, fading off in the distance. The woods were taking on their autumn color quickly now, and they took her breath away. God's beauty was constantly changing but neverendingly perfect.

Around the next bend in the lane, Molly caught sight of Lida and Becky heading for the schoolhouse. She waved.

Becky let go of Lida's hand and raced toward Molly, where she threw her arms around Molly's waist and squeezed. "We beat you. Lida said we would."

Molly hugged her, loving the feeling of the little arms around her. "You're a little early this morning. I thought I'd get to the inn before you left."

"We are going to wash the chalkboards this morning," Becky announced importantly. "So we have to be early."

"That's right." Lida reached them. "Don't worry. Leah and Aaron are having breakfast. I wanted to tell you that Leah insisted on moving from the bed to the wheelchair by herself this morning, and she did fine. She's getting daring, I think."

"What does that mean?" Becky switched over to Lida's hand.

Lida smiled at her. "It means she wants to try new things. That's good, but we'll have to keep an eye on her. And we'd best get on if we're going to have time to wash the boards."

Becky nodded, tugging at Lida's hand. "Yah, let's go."

Smiling at Becky's enthusiasm, Molly watched them disappear around the bend in the lane, marveling at the change in Becky today from the shy, withdrawn child she'd been on her arrival. She had changed so much. Surely, God must have arranged to bring Becky to the best place for her.

And Aaron as well? She felt a quiver in her midsection that said she didn't know whether to hope for that or not.

Nonsense, she told herself. It wasn't her business what Aaron wanted for the future. She could only hope it was the best for that little family.

Arriving at the inn, she and Leah started going over plans for the week, including the guests who'd be coming in for the wedding, followed by a full house for the weekend. Aaron had left early, planning to pick up the grocery order in town.

"Everyone is setting off early this morning, ain't so?" Leah gave her a questioning look. "You, too."

"Only because I knew Lida would be rushed after her first night here. Did everything go all right with her?"

"For sure," Leah said, looking pleased with herself. "Did she happen to mention what I did this morning?"

"Yah, she did," Molly responded. "Are you sure the doctor approved of you getting up by yourself? You know if you had fallen, Lida would have felt so guilty."

"But I didn't. And she didn't do anything wrong, so don't give her that idea."

"I wouldn't," she protested. "But when Mamm hears about it, she might not approve."

"She'll understand." Leah brushed away any such idea. "She'll know I have to try new things, or I'll start feeling sorry for myself. And there's nothing worse than that for any of us." Leah looked past her toward the screen door. "What brings your brother here this morning?"

Surprised, Molly went to the door as the pony cart pulled up at the porch. "Hey, what are you up to?"

Joshua grinned, pushing his straw hat back from his forehead. "I had other plans, but Mamm insisted I bring some apples over first." He leaned over so he could see Leah. "Just kidding, Leah. I'm happy to do it."

Joshua had always been one of Leah's favorites, so Molly wasn't surprised to see her give him an indulgent smile. "You'll have to come back when we've done some baking, yah?"

"I'll do that for sure." He switched his attention back to Molly. "How about giving me a hand putting these baskets away?"

Since he certain sure didn't need the help, Molly figured he had something private to say. Someone else who wanted to give her advice, she decided, and followed him out to the shed.

"I talked to Will after church…" he began, and she held up her hand in a stop motion.

"I already told him I don't care to talk to him just now, and if you don't want to get in trouble with me, you won't talk for him."

Josh was already shaking his head. "I won't. Hey, I'm on your side, always. I just wanted you to know that he hasn't given up."

Molly's heart seemed to swell. "Denke, Josh. You're a good brother."

He gave her a quick hug. "I always said I should have been the oldest," he said, grinning. "Just don't worry about Will. He'll give up. I could tell him to write you a letter."

"Good idea." The cloud that had been hanging over her head seemed to drift away. Her little bruder had made her feel better, as he always did.

Aaron drove back from town, hardly registering the colors that flowed down from the ridge to the valley. His thoughts were still roiling with the idea that had come to him. He had promised himself to put his daughter before everything else. He'd felt sure she felt as he did—that no one could take her mother's place. But with her simple whisper that she loved Molly, she had made him feel different about so many things.

Maybe the matchmakers were right. Maybe he and Molly could make a match of it, even if they couldn't forget their first loves. People married for a lot of reasons, didn't they?

Aaron's chest grew tight at the thought. The pony turned into the driveway and went on around to the kitchen door of the inn and suddenly he was convinced this was the right thing to do. Molly would see that, too. She'd realize that this was the best answer for all of them.

Suddenly eager to see Molly, he rushed through the job of unloading, responding automatically to his aunt's chatter. At last, nodding to something she'd said about the wedding on Thursday, he went in search of Molly. Now that he'd made up his mind, he wanted this settled.

He finally found her where he might have expected she'd be—in the office. She sat at the desk, seeming totally occupied in going over the schedule for the rest of the week. He stopped short of the doorway, watching her for a moment before she realized he was there.

She wore the forest green dress that brought out the deep russet color of her hair. A strand of that hair had slid out from beneath her kapp, and she brushed at it as if it were a fly flickering by her cheek. He moved, as if to tuck back the strand, and she saw him, her eyes growing wide.

"Aaron. Goodness, why didn't you say something? I didn't mean to ignore you." She pushed the schedule away with a quick gesture, a question in her eyes.

"You looked so busy I didn't want to interrupt."

Her lips curved. "This is your concern, too. It's going to be a busy week, ain't so?"

"For sure." It would be easy to slide into that conversation, but he'd made up his mind, and the sooner he said what he had come to say, the better. He took a deep breath. "There's something I wanted to suggest to you."

He ran out of both breath and words at the same time. Why hadn't he rehearsed this?

"Yah, of course." Molly gestured toward the chair opposite hers. "What is it?"

She was being helpful, while he stood there tongue-tied.

He slid into the chair and pulled it up a little so that they were knee to knee. "We should talk about the future…"

Molly's soft face seemed to tighten for a moment. Was she afraid of what the future might hold?

He cleared his throat and hoped he could explain without stumbling over his words. "It seems to me that it might be a good idea for us to get married." He rushed on. "Good for all of us, ain't so? Good for Aunt Leah, especially. She loves you, and she's taught you all she knows about running the inn. It would take me a lifetime to learn what you already know."

Her expression didn't encourage him, but he plunged on. "And besides, you have something else that I never will have, and that's a gift of hospitality. That's something God gave you, ain't so?"

"I hope so, but…"

He sensed something negative in her expression and was afraid she'd say no before he could convince her. "Don't you see that it's the perfect answer? You'll be here where you want to be, doing the job you love."

"Aaron." She grasped his hands and shook them as if to stop him. "Stop and think. Are you proposing or are you hiring a manager for the inn?"

He felt heat rush into his face. "Sorry. I didn't mean it to sound like that. It's just that I know you couldn't feel about me the way you felt about Will. And I… Well, I could never feel about anyone the way I felt about my wife. But people get married for other reasons, and we have some good reasons—Aunt Leah, the inn and Becky especially. She loves you, you know. I think it could be a good marriage. I would be faithful, and I'd never expect more than you want to give."

She pulled her hands free of his, shaking her head, and there was something in her face that convinced him it was no use.

"I'm sorry, Aaron. Everything you say is true, but it wouldn't work. I couldn't marry without love. You might think you could, but I would rather end my life as a maidal than do that. I'm sorry."

She seemed to choke on a sob, but before he could find something to convince her, she took a step back, stumbling a little on the chair as she turned. "Sorry," she murmured again, and hurried to the door and away.

He pushed himself up and stood looking at the empty doorway. He'd failed. What had he done wrong? Maybe he should have talked more about Becky, or about Aunt Leah.

And maybe the truth was that she couldn't stand the thought of being married to him. Maybe she still cherished thoughts of William, restored to the fold... William, wanting to marry her.

Molly hurried her steps, needing to avoid everyone until she regained control of herself. Other than Aaron, no one was here except Leah, but Leah... Leah had too much of an interest in her future. She didn't know Molly the way Mamm did, but right now she had her own plans for Molly's future. Maybe she'd even encouraged Aaron in his proposal.

Heat rushed up into her face at the very thought and she stopped, pressing her palms against her cheeks as she came to a halt outside the kitchen door. She could actually feel the warmth on her skin. She hated to think how red her face looked. Anyone who saw her would know something was wrong.

She could stay here in the hall...

No, she couldn't. She heard water running in the sink and the rattle of a pan. Leah must be there, probably tackling some of the apples Joshua had brought.

"Molly, is that you?" Leah's voice and the sound of the wheelchair sent panic rippling through her.

Moving silently, Molly slipped around to the back stairs and up toward the family bedrooms, leaving the noise behind her. Her heart slowed, and so did her breathing. It was all right. She could compose herself before she had to encounter anyone.

A moment later, she had slipped into Becky's room. She picked up a stuffed bear that had fallen from the bed onto the braided rug and hugged it against her chest. She sank down on the quilt. The bear comforted her, making her feel as if she were as young as Becky.

Don't think, she told herself. *Just breathe.*

That worked for a few breaths as her mind emptied out. But it couldn't last. As she calmed down, she inevitably began to go over again those moments with Aaron. How could he think that she would have found that an acceptable proposal? If he were hiring a housekeeper—

Shaking her head, she moved to the window, looking out at the smooth grass, still as green as it had been a month ago. A month ago, before Aaron had even appeared on her horizon, upsetting everything she thought she knew. And now, to crown it off, to propose marriage as if she would accept anyone who offered. She wasn't that desperate.

The sound of footsteps on the stairs had her spinning to the bed, putting the stuffed bear in place, just as Hilda called out. "Molly? Where are you?"

"Here. In Becky's room."

By the time Hilda opened the door, she was bent over

the bed, tucking the quilt into place over the pillows, her face hidden.

"This room looks fine, as usual," Hilda said. "And Leah is downstairs wanting some help with apples." Hilda smiled, reaching for Molly's hand and seeming to notice nothing. "You want to peel apples or finish whatever you're doing up here? I told her someone would be down soon." She looked at Molly. "Or do you want to go hide in the closet? I'll make an excuse for you."

So Hilda had noticed something was wrong.

"Denke, but I've heard your excuses before." That brought a real smile to her face. "Like the time I was late coming home from school, and you told my mamm I was chasing a lost pony. A lost pinto pony, ain't so? We didn't even know anyone with a pinto pony. Your imagination always goes flying when you tell stories."

"Well, it could have happened." Hilda caught her hand as if they were six years old again. "Komm on. If you want to talk, we could always go hang out some clothes."

"No, it's not a problem." Why was she letting it trouble her? She forced her lips into a smile and gave the quilt a final pat. "Let's go make apple cobbler or apple sauce or whatever."

They started down the stairs, but Molly couldn't stop wondering. What was it that made her get so ridiculously upset? She should have remained calm, just told Aaron that it wasn't a good plan, and kept her voice light and her face smiling.

Instead, she'd gotten upset and run away, and now Aaron was bound to think her reaction meant more than it did. And now it would be awkward between them and others would notice.

She let her hand slide down the stairway as she followed Hilda toward the kitchen, still turning the problem over and over in her mind. She certainly hadn't hurt Aaron's feelings. He didn't feel anything for her. The only thing she might have hurt was his pride.

And she… Her thoughts came to a halt. What about her feelings? Was it possible that her feelings had grown warmer for Aaron while they'd been working together?

She tried to sweep that thought away, but it wouldn't go. Was it possible?

So caught up in that idea, she didn't realize Hilda had stopped in front of her and Molly stepped on her heels. Hilda let out a squeak, Molly stumbled and Leah pushed open the swinging door.

"What are the two of you doing? We don't need anyone else around here having an accident. Where's Aaron? I thought he was with you, Molly."

Molly shook her head, sure she was red as a beet. Now what was she going to do about this? She couldn't possibly be feeling anything for Aaron. Could she?

Chapter Fourteen

Molly had managed to keep busy for the rest of the day, thanks to preparing for their incoming guests on Wednesday and Leah's desire to use up a whole basket of apples in one day. By the time Lida brought Becky and Dorie home from school, the whole house smelled of apple crumb pie, apple cobbler and walnut apple cake.

"Oh, yummy!" Dorie exclaimed as she and Becky burst in the kitchen door hand in hand. "I love apple cobbler. Especially with whipped cream."

"Dorie!" Molly and Lida said her name simultaneously. "You don't walk into someone's house," Molly continued, "and ask for something right away."

"Ach, nonsense," Leah said, holding out her arms to the girls. "They can have a piece. So long as you don't spoil your supper," she added to the two girls, who shook their heads instantly.

Molly glanced at Leah, thinking surely she wouldn't want to do the quilting they had planned after all that work. But Leah looked fresh as could be.

"Leah, wouldn't you like to take a little rest before supper? Lida and I can work with the girls on their quilts." Molly's tone was hopeful, but she suspected it wasn't going to work.

Sure enough, Leah shook her head with a brisk movement, looking up from hugging the girls. "Not a bit of it. We'll all have a snack first, and then we'll put in some time on our patches."

Soon, everyone was settled at the table with her choice of dessert. Becky looked around. "Isn't my daadi going to have some? He loves cobbler."

Molly tried to find an excuse, but Leah beat her to it. "He's painting the railing on the side porch. He'll want to finish that before he takes a break. Don't worry, there will be plenty for him. Ain't so, Molly?"

Molly jerked to attention. "Yah, for sure."

Becky seemed satisfied, but Molly's stomach fluttered. Had Leah done that deliberately? She couldn't help thinking that Leah must have guessed that something had happened between her and Aaron. Either that or she knew.

Maybe Aaron had told her what he intended. If so, she'd... Well, she didn't know what she'd do, but she'd think of something. And if she continued to jump whenever Aaron was mentioned, everyone would know something had happened, anyway.

The girls finished their snacks and got their sewing out quickly. Leaning over to peek at Becky's stitches, Dorie shook her head. "You're only on your second patch, and I'm on my third already." Then she caught Molly frowning at her and tried to pretend she hadn't spoken.

Molly sighed and tilted her little sister's face back toward hers. "What would Mammi say if she heard you say that?"

"Not to do it," Dorie muttered. "I'm sorry." She leaned over and looked again. "Yours is neater than mine, anyway."

Molly's gaze met Lida's, and her lips twitched. It was going to take every female member of the family to get through to Dorie. She certain sure had enough confidence for any three children.

Once Dorie had been chastened for the moment, the sewing went smoothly, and so did the conversation. The little girls told them all about school that afternoon, and even recited the poem they were learning about autumn…the same one Molly had learned a few years earlier.

Feeling considerably settled down, Molly got up. "I'll go out and harness the pony and cart. Joshua left it for us after he dropped off the apples."

"Do you want me to?" Lida started to get up, but Molly waved her back.

The sooner she got moving, the better. This way, she'd be able to leave for home before Aaron came back inside. She didn't want to see him again today.

Once on her way to the stable, Molly felt a sense of relief. By tomorrow, the memory of Aaron's proposal would be fading, and she would be able to face him. She slid the stable door back and blinked at the dimness inside. A shadowy figure pushed up from a straw bale and stepped toward her. If Aaron had decided to bring the subject up again…

It wasn't Aaron. It was Will. Her first instinct was to turn around and speed back out of the stable. But she'd already done that once today in the face of something challenging, and she wouldn't do it again.

"Will. What are you doing here?" Molly stiffened her spine, planting herself firmly on the spot. She belonged here—Will didn't.

"Waiting for you." He came a couple of steps closer. "I said we had to talk."

"And I said I didn't want to talk." If that wasn't just like

Will. Always sure he could get what he wanted with that sweet smile. Well, she wasn't in the mood to be sweet-talked.

"Ach, Molly, come on. We're old friends. You can't refuse to talk to me." He reached out as if to take her hand, and she jerked back.

"Watch me," she snapped. "You were gone a long time. We don't have anything to say to each other."

His smile seemed to get forgotten on his face. "We could talk about old times, like the fun we used to have."

"Like the time you talked me into climbing on the roof of the shed and Daad had to bring the ladder to get me down?" She could still remember how scared she'd been.

"At least I ran and got your daad, didn't I? And he chewed me out. And my daad took the switch to me."

"You deserved it."

He shrugged. "I usually did."

"You mean you usually talked your way out of things." She had to hide a smile at the memory of those times.

"Not with you, ain't so? You could always see through me. Komm on," he said, his face crinkling. "Admit it. My running away was the best thing that ever happened to you."

"I didn't see it that way at the time."

"But it was, wasn't it?" He seemed determined not to look ashamed. "We were good friends, but we'd have been a terrible married couple. Admit it."

Molly was ready to snap back at him, but she couldn't. A smile was tugging at her lips. "Couldn't you have found a better way of telling me that at the time?"

Will's expression relaxed. "Not then. I never was good at taking the blame for anything. You knew that better than anybody. Forgive me?"

"I guess so." The smile won. "You would have been a terrible husband."

"But a gut friend, yah?"

She nodded. "Now how about getting out of here so I can get on with my work?" She shooed him toward the open door.

Will patted her on the shoulder, leaned forward, and kissed her cheek lightly. "Denke, Molly. See you soon."

Turning toward the harness rack, Molly realized someone was standing at the back door. He looked back over his shoulder, evidently talking with his aunt. She let out a sigh of relief... Thank goodness he hadn't looked out a little sooner, or he might have seen her with Will. She didn't know why that was such a relief, but she'd rather he didn't see her with Will.

He should be happy for Molly, Aaron told himself. From the look of her and Will together, she was getting her first choice, after all. She'd probably be happy and excited when she came in.

So why didn't he feel that way for her? It didn't make any sense to be standing here like a pillar of salt with his stomach churning. He hurried back into the kitchen. Somehow, he didn't want to hear her say that she and Will had patched their relationship together again. Well, she'd been avoiding him all day and now he'd avoid her. Nobody would know why.

"Aunt Leah, I finished painting the side porch. Turned out pretty good, I think."

"Gut, gut." She looked pleased, and he wondered if she was relieved to have him here to take on some of the responsibility.

"Let's go see!" Grabbing Becky's hand, Dorie rushed to the door. Just in time, Aaron grabbed the two of them.

"Not yet. It has to dry. We don't want little fingerprints all over it."

"How do you know we'd do that?" Dorie looked up at him as if she really did want to know, making him grin.

"Because I was your age once," he responded. "Fresh paint and fresh concrete are irresistible."

Dorie was looking at him as if doubting that he'd really been her age ever. But she nodded.

"Look, here comes Molly," Leah said. "You can help carry that big pan of cobbler out to the cart."

He couldn't very well dash off without helping, so his idea of avoiding Molly was doomed to failure. He'd have to pretend he hadn't seen anything. He picked up the pan of cobbler, beating Lida to it.

"I'll take this. You get the door."

Lida nodded, not having any idea how much he'd like to leave it to her.

When they all got outside, the sun was nearly down to the tree line to the west, glaring in their eyes. Molly slid down from the pony cart, shielding her eyes with her hand.

"Cobbler for your family," he said, lifting the pan in a gesture.

"Ach, that's so nice. You didn't have to share that."

Aunt Leah rushed to answer. "We wanted to. And besides, Joshua would be disappointed, ain't so?"

Molly smiled, chuckling a little. "Joshua is always disappointed to miss something sweet, you know that."

"Everybody knows that," Lida said emphatically. She gave her little sister a boost up to the cart.

Dorie waved vigorously, nearing hitting Lida on the nose.

"Bye, Leah. Bye, Becky. Bye, Aaron. I'll see you tomorrow."

And by tomorrow, Aaron thought, she'd have heard she was going to have a new brother-in-law. He'd been assuming Molly would come in and tell Aunt Leah first, but naturally she'd want her own parents to be the first to know.

He should be happy for her. He *was* happy for her. After all, it wasn't her fault their situations weren't so alike, after all. She'd lost her first love and then found him again. It wasn't that way for him. He let out a long breath.

He'd miss her when she left, but they'd find a replacement. Maybe Hilda would like to work full-time.

Even as he thought it, he knew he couldn't listen to Hilda's chatter all day long. There had to be a better solution. He scooped Becky up in his arms so she could watch Molly drive away. He relaxed as she went out of view, and they headed to the kitchen.

Now if Becky had something to do, he could talk to Aunt Leah about it. She might not be happy, but she did know the families well, and he knew she'd given some thought to this happening.

Sure enough, Becky darted off toward her bedroom, and Aaron poured a mug of coffee from the pot on the stove.

"Did you see Will out at the stable with Molly?" he asked abruptly.

Aunt Leah's eyes grew wide with shock. "Will? No! I had no idea that he was here. What was he doing?"

Obviously, she hadn't seen.

"He was kissing her." He was surprised with himself. He hadn't meant to blurt that out. "So I guess we'll have to hire someone to take her place, yah?"

She shook her head. "I can't believe it."

"What can't you believe? That they've made up? Or that she's still ready to marry him again?" The dislike in his voice startled him, but there it was.

Aunt Leah's gaze rested on his face, considering. "You didn't like it when I wanted you and Molly to get together. Now that it seems she's found someone else, you don't like that either, ain't so?"

Aaron stared at her, speechless. He didn't have an answer, so he walked out of the room.

Molly and her sisters were squeezed into the seat of the pony cart, and as usual Dorie was wiggling in the middle. "I like working on the quilt. It won't take very long to finish it. And you know what?"

"No, what?" At least with Dorie asking questions every two minutes, Molly realized she was too occupied to think about anything else…like Aaron or Will.

"Aaron was teasing me. I think that means he likes me. Whenever somebody teases you, they like you. I figured that out."

Lida gave her a quick squeeze. "Listen to who knows all about men and women."

"Well, she might be right," Molly said, smiling at them.

"See?" Dorie sounded as if she knew it all.

"Sassy," Lida said. "You'd better not let Daadi hear you say that. You know he doesn't like it."

Dorie clapped her hand over her lips and looked from one sister to the other. "I didn't mean to. Sometimes it just bubbles up in me and comes out before I can stop it."

Molly didn't dare look at Lida for fear they'd both laugh at her. After a moment to gain control, Molly said, "Try harder."

When they pulled into the yard and up to the back porch, Dorie grabbed at the reins. "Me, me. I'll drive to the barn."

"Lida will help you," Molly said firmly. "I'll take the cobbler in."

And maybe she'd get a few minutes alone with Mammi. She felt she could use that just now.

"Cobbler," she announced, setting it on the counter and looking over her mother's shoulder at the chicken and dumplings she was stirring gently on the stove. "What can I do to help?"

"Looks like you've had a busy day already." Her mother gave her a quick hug, and then looked at her face again. "Was ist letz?"

Molly took a step back, blinking. "What makes you think something's wrong?"

Mammi just smiled. She always knew when something was wrong. Molly realized she shouldn't even try.

"Nothing's really wrong. Not now. I had a talk with Will, just like you said. And just like you said, we're okay." She tried to dismiss Aaron from her thoughts.

"Gut." Her mother gave her a quick squeeze. "You did the right thing." Mamm hesitated. "But there's something else, ain't so?"

Molly thought briefly about Aaron's proposal and yanked her thoughts away from it. She shook her head.

"I'll set the table. The girls are taking care of the pony and cart."

Mamm watched her for several minutes and then patted her cheek. "Tell me when you want to."

Lifting the plates from the cabinet, Molly tried to pretend she hadn't heard, but it didn't seem to work. Aaron's voice sounded in her thoughts again, saying they should get married, saying it would be the best thing to do, but leaving out the most important thing.

She set the plates on the table and looked again at her mother. "How do you know?"

"I've been listening to you since you were born. I can tell when something isn't right. You'll be the same when you have kinder."

Molly brushed away a tear from her cheek. "I'm beginning to think that will never happen." She sucked in a deep breath and let the words burst out. "Aaron asked me to marry him this morning. He said it would be best for everyone. He told me all the things that made it a good idea…his aunt, my relationship with Becky, her need for a mother, running the inn together. Then he said he didn't love me, but that was okay."

She had an urge to stamp her feet on the floor and slam something on the table. "I was so angry with him I wanted to throw something. How could he?"

"People can say foolish things sometimes, especially when they're not sure what they want." Mammi patted her hand.

"It was foolish all right." She shook her head. "How could he say that?"

"I'm sure he's sorry now."

"He should be," Molly muttered. She turned away and reached for the silverware. "As if I would marry someone who didn't love me."

"Of course, you wouldn't," she said comfortingly. "All the same… I don't think you'd be so angry if you didn't have feelings for him."

Molly stared at her. Then she shook her head. "The only feeling I have for Aaron is annoyance. Nothing more."

Chapter Fifteen

The next day began smoothly for Molly. Her mother didn't say anything more about her feelings for Aaron, and when she arrived at the inn, Aaron himself avoided talking to her, finding some outside chores to keep him busy. That suited Molly just fine. She didn't want any more surprises. She'd had enough the previous day.

Certainly, she had plenty to keep her busy, with the wedding guests coming in tomorrow, followed by a full house on the weekend. After checking the guest rooms, she started to go down the stairs for fresh sheets and spotted Leah at the bottom with sheets and pillowcases stacked on her lap.

Leah, apparently not paying attention to her, reached up to the railing with one hand.

"Leah! What are you doing?" Molly came close to a shout as she hurried down.

Leah glanced up, her face like one of the kinder who'd been caught doing something wrong.

"Nothing." She sounded just like one of them, too.

Molly's heart was still pounding when she reached her. "It looked as if you were trying to pull yourself up the stairs. You know you're not ready for that yet."

"Ach, I'm tired of this." She smacked her hand down on the arm of the wheelchair. "I can do more. I'm not a baby."

Kneeling at her side, Molly knew she had to choose her words carefully. Leah was just the person to do what others said she couldn't, like running the inn by herself. But not this time.

"I know," she said gently. "And you are doing wonderful gut. Everyone says so. But bones don't heal very quickly, especially…" She let that trail off.

"Especially when you're old," Leah snapped. Then, before Molly could say anything, Leah caught her hand. "Ach, I'm sorry. I'm just a foolish old woman."

"You are not." Molly's lips twitched. "You know you'd be just as lively as my mamm if you hadn't fallen."

Leah never was able to feel sorry for herself for long, and a smile just touched her lips. "Well, I'm not so sure of that. I've got a few years up on your mamm. But you're right. I'll try to behave. Sorry."

Molly studied her face, wondering what had happened to make Leah so feisty this morning. She certain sure hoped Leah wasn't going to start hinting again at making a match. She'd heard enough from others on that subject.

Just then Leah turned enough to see out the side window. "Look, there's Aaron coming in. Let's stop for a cup of coffee."

Molly scooped up the armload of sheets and pillow-cases. "I'll get these beds made first," she said, and fled back upstairs.

When she was securely behind the closed door of the largest guest room, Molly sank into a rocking chair, holding the armful of bedding. Leaning back, she admitted she was doing worse instead of better. Anyone would think she'd lost her heart to Aaron, and that wouldn't be true. Yes, she liked him, and she'd been hurt when he thought they should marry without love. But she had to get ahold of herself.

A rap came on the door, and it started to open. Molly shot out of the chair, dropping a pair of pillowcases in the process. She bent to pick them up and barely missed colliding with Aaron as he did the same.

"Sorry!" He caught her with one hand and scooped up the sheets with the other. "Did I bump you?"

"No, no. I'm all right." She brushed her palm across her forehead. "Did you need something?"

"Just to give you a hand with these." Grasping the sheets as well, he took everything over to the bed and began shaking them out. "Aunt Leah says we should finish with these and then go have coffee."

"And a cruller," Molly added, remembering.

"Crullers?" His eyes lit up. "We have crullers?"

"My mamm sent them," she said in explanation. "She believes that a dish should never be returned empty. But I can do the sheets in a jiffy."

Shaking his head, he let the sheet billow out over the bed. Molly grabbed the other side automatically and stretched it tight.

"We'll do them together in half a jiffy, yah?" His face relaxed in a smile, his eyes crinkling.

"I guess we will."

Aaron's smile had her heart tumbling. Molly focused on the job at hand, trying to get her thoughts in order. She had turned down his proposal the previous day for a very good reason. She wouldn't marry without love, even if he would.

"Komm on," he said impatiently, straightening the top sheet.

"All right, all right." She tried not to focus on the smile. Tried not to see the crinkled corners of his eyes. Her heart thudded in her chest, and once again she felt the fluttering that she couldn't dismiss. Her mother's words slipped through her mind again. Was it possible she actually did have feelings for Aaron?

For a moment, she held on to that thought, looking at it from every angle. Then, as if she'd missed a step, she knew what she'd been hiding from herself. This wasn't the feeling she'd had for Will. No, it was bigger, and deeper, and more real. Aaron was a person who'd already been through life's trials and challenges and who relied on strength and faith to see him through, not charm.

With him and Becky, they could have a strong, loving family. But it wouldn't happen. He had already told her— he'd never love anyone but his late wife.

She touched the double wedding ring quilt lightly and then turned to the door. "We'd better go downstairs. Leah will be waiting."

The crullers were every bit as good as Aaron had anticipated. He'd gotten back to work quickly, trying to stay out of Molly's way. Now it was nearly time for Becky to come home from school, and he felt stuffed as well as apprehensive. Molly had still, as far as he could see, not mentioned her future plans to Aunt Leah. Didn't she see how unfair that was? If she planned to marry soon, she'd want to be free of her job. Surely, that was what Will wanted. They'd wasted too much time already.

If Molly didn't want to, maybe he should at least hint to Aunt Leah. It would be hard enough for her to adjust to life without Molly. It would be worse if the news caught her by surprise. She'd want time to come to a decision about Molly's replacement, and with all the reservations they had for the next month, time was one thing they didn't have.

Feeling determined to have something settled, he would at least sound Aunt Leah out about the possibility. He headed for the kitchen, thinking he'd find her there.

He'd been right, but he hadn't thought about how he'd bring up the subject, especially when his aunt looked up with a happy smile at his approach.

"There you are. I was starting to wonder." Aunt Leah gestured toward the coffeepot on the stove. "Sit down. Have some coffee and tell me why you and Molly are avoiding each other."

Ignoring the coffee, Aaron planted his hands on the back of the nearest chair. "What makes you think that?"

He was immediately sorry he'd asked the question. It had been the perfect opening, and he'd flubbed it. "Ach, that was a silly thing to say. It's been obvious, ain't so?"

"Yah." His aunt studied his face. "Are you going to tell me? I thought you two were getting along much better lately. Maybe you'd even started to…"

He hurried into speech before she could say it. "You'll have to forget whatever you've been thinking about the two of us making a match."

"I wasn't matchmaking," she protested, but without much assurance in her voice. "But you do like each other, so why not?"

The words were on the tip of his tongue, and they came out before he could stop them. "Because I already asked her, and she said no."

"Why? What did you do?"

"It wasn't my fault." He was indignant that she automatically blamed him. "It was too late. It was too late from the time Will came home."

Aunt Leah gaped at him for a moment and then shook her head. "You're wrong. She had no intention of going back to Will. She told me so."

His jaw tightened so much he thought he couldn't say a word, but he got it out. "Have you seen them together since worship? Well, I have. I saw them out by the barn together, and I saw them kiss. And if that doesn't mean they're back together again, I don't know what does." He took advantage of her speechlessness to go on. "Besides, she told me herself that she'd never marry without love. So we'd best figure out how to replace her."

There, it was said. At least his aunt knew, and they would have to look toward a future that didn't have Molly in it.

Waving goodbye to Lida, Molly turned back toward the house. Becky was probably already having her after-school snack. She'd run into the house quickly, saying something about showing Aunt Leah her arithmetic paper. That had made her smile, satisfied that Leah was taking her place in Becky's life.

To her surprise, Becky wasn't in the kitchen, but the atmosphere between Leah and Aaron was tense. It must have been enough to send Becky scurrying, and it seemed to be having the same effect on her.

But before she could make an excuse to leave, the picture broke up as Leah swung her chair around to the stove and Aaron, muttering something, brushed past her on his way out the back door.

Now what? she wondered. She hesitated for a moment

and then suppressed the urge to skip out on the problem, whatever it might be. "What's wrong?"

Leah swung back around to face her. "Why didn't you tell me that Aaron asked you to marry him?"

It was said in such an accusing manner that Molly couldn't find a reply for a moment. Then her head came up. "Because it was private," she said firmly. She wasn't going to apologize for not sharing everything with Leah. That wasn't part of their friendship. She saw that get through to Leah. Her expression changed, and the older woman brushed a hand across her forehead.

"Yah, I guess that's true enough. But if I'd known, I might not have said the wrong thing to Aaron."

Molly could see the reluctance in her face—it was part of Leah's confidence that she seldom if ever admitted she was wrong. Molly waited another moment, and then she sighed. "Have you been matchmaking again?"

"No!" The denial was a little too fast. "Well, not exactly. It's just… I thought it felt so right. And then Aaron announced you were going to marry Will, and that we'd have to replace you."

Molly pressed her palm against her stomach, which seemed to be spinning like a child's top. "What? I hope he hasn't been telling people that because it's not true."

"But he said he saw you…saw you and Will," she gestured vaguely toward the backyard. "He saw you kissing him in the barn."

"He didn't," Molly protested.

"I did." Aaron spoke from the doorway.

Molly swung on him. "What you saw wasn't me kissing him. It was Will kissing me. A friend's kiss on the cheek, to thank me for forgiving him."

She stopped, looking around and suddenly realizing something that was far more important than what Aaron understood. "Where is Becky?"

"Not home yet," Leah said.

Molly began shaking her head and couldn't seem to stop. "I was talking to Lida in the yard. Becky hurried inside at least fifteen minutes ago, eager to start on her sewing."

She could see the realization hit Aaron's face. "She heard. She must have." He looked from her to his aunt as if not knowing who to blame. "Where is she?"

Her hand fisted against her stomach. "She's gone. We have to find her. Quickly."

Aaron was already heading for the door. "I'll look outside. You two check in here. She has to understand it's not her fault."

The screen door banged behind him, and Molly raced for the stairs. He was right about one thing, even though he was wrong about so much else. Becky would blame herself, and all the good changes of her time here would be wiped out in a minute.

Chapter Sixteen

Molly heard Leah's chair rolling into her bedroom while she raced for the stairs. Aaron had been sensible to take the outside to search while they did the inside, but she couldn't help but feel sure Becky would be inside the house. She wasn't comfortable yet exploring the outside unless she was with Dorie. No, she'd be looking for a little hiding place where she might feel safe.

Reaching the next floor, she paused to catch her breath and steady herself. No running wildly through the house. Becky would already be upset enough if she had overheard what they thought she had. They shouldn't upset her more. Children relied on the adults in their lives to stay calm.

Only Molly wasn't calm, not inside. Her heart was pounding so hard she could almost see it. Poor child. Becky wouldn't know what to think. She probably saw her life being turned upside down again.

Aaron had caused this with his habit of jumping to conclusions. How could he assume she would go back to William? Hadn't she been clear that she wasn't?

Leaving the chance of going back to Will out of it, she didn't know whether there would be chances for them, anyway. Not of her making, that was certain sure.

What did Aaron want in his future? Not her, for sure.

Molly searched Aaron's room slowly and carefully, checking every place that was large enough to hide a small girl. A child Becky's age didn't take up much space. Like a typical Amish bedroom, the room was plain and simple, with only one chest of drawers and a row of pegs on the wall. A bookcase and a low shelf, along with a spool bed, completed the furnishings.

It didn't take long. As she went out, she paused in the doorway and said Becky's name. "Becky, are you here? I just want to talk to you."

Her head tilted, she scanned the room. Nothing. But then, somewhere nearby, there was a sound…a sound she hadn't expected to hear in an empty room.

Molly froze, puzzled. "Becky, please tell me where you are. We need to talk."

No answer. But after a moment, the sound came again— a scraping noise. Not in this room, but maybe in the adjoining room, the one belonging to Becky.

She hurried to Becky's bedroom, hesitating for a second. Call for Aaron? No, not until she was sure, and not until she heard what exactly Becky was thinking.

Standing just inside the room, Molly looked and listened. As her gaze moved around the room, her heart gave a thud. She knew what the sound had been. The sound of the latch on the hidden closet.

Of course, the logical place for any child to hide. She crossed to the closet quietly, reaching for the outside latch. Praying silently, she tried to open it. Nothing resulted. It wouldn't move. Becky must have moved the latch so at it stuck in the wrong position.

Molly pressed her palm against the door, putting her lips

close to the crack. "Becky, please, sweet girl. Unlock the door. We need to talk."

"I don't want to." Becky's voice was choked with tears. "I can't."

"For sure you can," Molly said calmly. "I think you heard something that you didn't understand. Maybe together we can figure it out, ain't so?"

Becky sniffled a little. "No. I can't."

"It'll be better if we talk, I promise you."

"No… I mean, I can't open it. Something's wrong with the lock." Her voice trembled, and Molly could hear the fear in it. "It won't open." Her voice rose.

"Don't be frightened. Nothing is going to hurt you. I'll go call Daadi—"

"No, no, I can't talk to him." A sob punctuated the words. "He wouldn't understand. He never talks about Mammi."

Molly's throat seemed to freeze, and for a moment she didn't think she could say a word. She'd thought this was about the idea of her marrying and leaving, but apparently it wasn't.

"I don't understand." Becky almost wailed. "Did he forget Mammi?"

There was a step, and Molly, sitting on her heels next to the closet, turned to see Aaron about to come in. She signaled for quiet. Becky had to tell them what was going on, but she feared if Becky realized her daadi was there, she'd clam up.

"I'm sure he didn't forget, Becky. Some people find it hard to talk about a person they loved who has passed."

"But I need to talk about her," Becky protested. "I might forget if I don't. I don't ever want to forget my mammi. And I don't want to lose you, either. I love you, Molly." The words were broken with a sob.

"Oh, sweet girl." Molly's own voice shook as she fought to keep from crying. Glancing at Aaron's face, she realized he was on the verge of tears himself. "I'm not going anywhere. I'm not getting married." She kept herself from looking at Aaron again. "Daadi was just mixed up about it. I'll be right here as long as you want me."

"Are you sure?" Becky's voice sounded suspicious. Apparently, she'd heard too many things that weren't true.

"Certain sure." She kept her tone light.

Aaron reached out to touch the door. "I'm sorry, Becky. I... I thought it was better to keep still about Mammi. I thought it would make you sad to talk about her. But I'll tell you anything you want. I promise."

The silence seemed to last forever. Then the latch wiggled. Molly pulled it back on her side, Aaron gave it a yank and Becky tumbled out into his arms.

Molly sat back on the floor, leaning against the closet door. Every bit of energy was wiped out of her. Aaron looked as if he felt the same. He held Becky against him, and her tears were dampening his shirt.

No, she didn't have enough left to feel anything. Somehow, she'd have to find a way to mother Becky, take care of Leah and deal with a man she loved but who didn't love her and never would.

Aaron was relieved when Lida and the twins turned up after supper. Becky had begun to seem normal again, and this would prove a good distraction for her. He went outside with the children and got the four of them playing a game involving lots of running, shouting and hiding. He suspected it was good for him, too.

He stood, watching them run. Dorie was in the lead, her

hair pulling loose from her kapp and hanging in a braid on one side. Lida was trying to get her attention, but it didn't help. David and Becky closed in on Dorie, one on each side, but she put on a spurt and got away from them.

Aaron glanced around, not seeing Molly. He hadn't had a chance to say a thing to her after they'd found Becky. He'd been too preoccupied with Becky's needs. But he had to. She deserved better from him. She'd done so much for his family, and he hadn't shown much faith in her. Molly deserved more.

Maybe she had gone into the house. He signaled to Lida that he was going into the kitchen, and she nodded. She'd keep an eye on the young ones, of course.

He reached the kitchen, still not sure what he was going to say to her. But Aunt Leah was alone there. She glanced at him, her graying eyebrows lifting. "Was ist letz? What's wrong?"

"Didn't Molly come in? I need to talk to her, to tell her I'm sorry for misunderstanding."

She didn't look very impressed at his plans for atonement. "I should think you do. What were you thinking? How could you ask her to marry you and at the same time tell her you didn't love her?"

He gave an exasperated sigh. "You're the one who wanted our marriage so much. I couldn't lie to her about my feelings."

His aunt looked at him for a long moment. "What do you feel for Molly?" The question contained a challenge he didn't understand.

"Well, I admire her. You know that, ain't so? She's good at everything she does. Kind, reliable and patient. I care about her, and I want her to be happy. But I don't feel like I did for my wife. That was love."

His aunt shook her head. "That was first love—an up in the air exhilaration that's like nothing else. No, you can't go back and have that again. But love is different every time."

She said that so passionately he wondered if she had felt love again since his uncle passed. He longed to ask her, but he didn't dare.

He wasn't sure he believed her, anyway. How could what he felt for Molly be truly love?

He shook his head. "I don't know. I'd have to think about it."

"Well, don't think so long that you lose her entirely," she snapped. She swung her chair away from him.

The back door burst open, and Dorie rushed in, followed closely by Becky.

"Somebody help!" Dorie exclaimed.

Becky pushed past her. "Daadi, do something. Molly is out at the barn. She's crying."

"Molly never cries." Dorie couldn't get the words out fast enough. "Never. Somebody has to help."

"I'll take care of Molly." He caught both girls before they could run out and pushed them gently toward Aunt Leah. "You two stay here with Aunt Leah. This is my job."

He ran out, not thinking anything through, only knowing that this was his job. Anything to do with Molly was his job, his responsibility, his joy or his sorrow.

Molly evidently hadn't realized the kinder had seen her. She stood near the stall door, leaning against it, her face bent against the curve of her arm on the wooden bar, shoulders shaking a little.

Aaron didn't stop to think…he just raced toward her, put

his arms around her and pulled her close against him. She didn't resist, didn't say anything. She just leaned against his chest and let her tears soak into his shirt.

He put his cheek against her temple, feeling her soft hair against his skin, knowing he'd come home. "I'm sorry," he murmured. "I've done all the wrong things, but I truly love you, Molly. Can you forgive me?"

Molly nodded slightly, her arms slipping around him even as his lips found hers. She responded readily, and he knew the truth of what his aunt had said. This was love, true love. Different from what he'd felt before, but just as deep and sure and filled with a passion that amazed him.

After what seemed like an eternity, Molly pulled back a little, looking into his eyes. Her own were filled with so much love that it humbled him. This was right. It couldn't be anything else.

A smile teased her lips. "Did you change your mind about marrying again?"

He felt a rumble of laughter inside. "Only if it's you," he said. "Let's see how soon the bishop will marry us. Then we can start on our lives together."

"You and me and Becky. And your aunt. And whatever babies we have together."

His heart swelled at the very thought of it. God had breached his stubborn heart by bringing him together with the perfect person for him.

He heard a small rustle of sound. "We have an audience," he whispered, and she looked toward the door.

Lida stood there, holding all three kinder so firmly that they couldn't move a step. He felt a bubble of laughter and didn't know if it was in himself or in Molly. But he looked at Lida and nodded slightly.

Obediently, Lida released the young ones, and they came scrambling to throw themselves against them.

"Are you all right?" Becky asked anxiously.

"Why were you crying, Molly?" Dorie tugged at her skirt, wanting an answer.

"She doesn't want to talk to us right now," David told his twin. "She's busy."

"But I want to know."

"Because she's happy," Lida said, rounding them up and drawing them away. "Come on. We'll go tell Leah." All of them started running for the house. Becky lingered a moment to wrap her arms as far around them as she could and then ran after the others.

Aaron felt himself smile before he kissed Molly again. Then he drew back. "I think I know the difference between a friend kiss and a lover's kiss. This was a lover's kiss. I love you, Molly. Now and forever."

She nodded and let out a trembling breath. "Yah," she whispered. "Forever."

* * * * *

If you enjoyed this story,
don't miss the previous books in the
Brides of Lost Creek series from Marta Perry:

Second Chance Amish Bride
The Wedding Quilt Bride
The Promised Amish Bride
The Amish Widow's Heart
A Secret Amish Crush
Nursing Her Amish Neighbor
The Widow's Bachelor Bargain

Find more great reads at www.LoveInspired.com

Dear Reader,

How nice it is to be coming back to you with another Lost Creek story. The Amish Inn has been mentioned in several books, and I thought it was time to give it a bigger role. I've had a picture of it in my mind for a long time, and I hope you'll be able to see it as well.

Have you ever noticed how a sudden accident can change everything? When I fell and broke my hip last fall, I lay there holding my husband's hand and waiting for the ambulance. I felt the world spinning around me, and all of the busyness that had filled my mind just the moment before, including writing this book, just vanished. If I could, I would have carried on with all the things I had to do, but God had other plans for me...like making new friends in the hospital and the rehab center. Like letting other people help me and being truly grateful to them. Like turning to God for the strength and wisdom to get through each day.

My life is a little different now, and I certainly knew how Leah felt to be stuck in bed and completely reliant on others!

I hope that you don't experience any such accident, but if you do, you can rely on God to be standing beside you, holding your hand all the way.

Blessings,
Marta Perry